If Every Month Were June

If Every Month Were June

a novel by **Tony Bender**

FULCRUM
GOLDEN, COLORADO

This is a work of fiction. Names, characters, places, or incidents
either are the product of the author's imagination or are used
fictitiously.

Library of Congress Cataloging-in-Publication Data

Bender, Tony, 1958-
  If every month were June / Tony Bender.
     p. cm.
  ISBN-13: 978-1-55591-684-8
  ISBN-13: 978-1-55591-660-2 (pbk.)
  1. Sexual attraction--Fiction. I. Title.
  PS3602.E465I44 2008
  813'.6--dc22
                                    2007051818

Printed in the United States of America by Malloy Incorporated
0 9 8 7 6 5 4 3 2 1

Design by Margaret McCullough
Cover model Gabby West, represented by ckwestmedia@aol.com,
courtesy of Mindas Photography, www.mindas.com

Fulcrum Publishing
4690 Table Mountain Drive, Suite 100
Golden, Colorado 80403
800-992-2908 • 303-277-1623
www.fulcrumbooks.com

This one's for The Redhead, for believing in me.

"Even as women run deep as a pristine blue ocean, men are shallow, muddy puddles with drowned worms at the bottom."

—*If Every Month Were June*

"No person can make another person happy. But one person can surely make another miserable."

—Rabbi Goldberg

chapter One

It wasn't stalking. Not really.

It was love. It really was. A love like that can't be criminal. It was worship, and in America freedom of religion is guaranteed by the Constitution.

Hooter Pridley never really penciled it out in his head that way. But if he had, that's how he would have rationalized it. Hooter was no dummy. He just wasn't deep. He was like a water bug skittering across the surface of thought. Once in a while he would dive in and mull things over, but soon he was back on the surface, zipping from one whim to another.

No one would have taken him seriously if he had said he was in love with a woman he had never met. A woman he had never even heard speak. Those weren't the sorts of things any self-respecting fellow told anyone. Hooter shared it all with his diary—which you might think is a sissified thing for a man to do. That's what Hooter thought, until he discovered that his grandpa kept a diary, and Grandpa was no sissy. But his diary contained such entries as *We put in three hundred acres of soybeans today* or *The hail knocked down all the soybeans today*. That sort of thing. Hooter, on the other hand, shared his innermost feelings.

He was smitten the first time he saw her, but when he saw her again a few months later at the Kum and Go convenience store newsstand out along the interstate, he realized it was destiny.

It's destiny, he wrote in his diary that day, along with a bunch of other stuff about carburetors, torque wrenches, and glass pack mufflers.

Hooter was the head parts man at Wangdoodle Auto & Truck Parts in Sterling, Colorado. Sounds pretty, doesn't it—*Sterling, Colorado.*

"Bet the mountains are something to see," folks would say to Hooter when he traveled—which wasn't often.

"Don't have any mountains in Sterling," Hooter would say.

"That's the shits."

Hooter would agree that it was, indeed, the shits.

People got the idea from Coors beer commercials that Colorado was all mountains. Hooter supposed that some people actually believed that big horses delivered all the Budweiser too. Hooter wasn't deep, but he knew that advertising was "horse hockey," as his grandpa would say. Whatever that meant.

Hooter saw those ads in the magazines—the ones with young, taut-bodied, tanned couples skipping barefoot down the beach, every one of them with a cigarette in their hand. The message was implicit: *Smoking makes you beautiful. Cigarettes are an integral part of any successful exercise regimen. Chicks dig it.* But the only smokers Hooter ever knew were wrinkled and too busy hacking up chunks of their lungs to skip more than a few feet along the beach before collapsing and being washed out to sea, never to be seen again.

Not that Hooter was a pessimist. He had started smoking himself for a while, even though he had a girlfriend, a darn nice one, too. Although he never gave it a whole lot of thought, in the back of his mind he figured that if he smoked enough, he might get an even better girlfriend.

That's how all of this got started—with a vague sense of dissatisfaction in his subconscious. R. J. Reynolds might have put it there. Who knows? Wouldn't it be ironic if some advertising guy in Manhattan made him feel empty inside and set him off bouncing around against other people and upsetting their lives too? What if advertising did that to people? That would be the shits. Or horse hockey, at least.

In the unlikely event that Hooter came to that conclusion, he never would have blamed anyone but himself. Hooter had this quaint idea, which he got from his folks, that he should take responsibility for his own actions—even if someone else told him to run amuck. It all goes back to jumping off a bridge. If your friends did something like that, would you? Heck no! Not unless it was a low bridge and the water was warm. And you could swim.

Folks don't take much personal responsibility anymore. That was a passing fad. These days, if a klutz spills hot coffee in his lap, he sues. But the coffee didn't spill itself. Coffee is generally well behaved. Everyone knows the deal with coffee: it's hot, and it keeps you awake. Especially if you pour it on your crotch. Why do we need lawyers and judges to sort it out? Because folks don't take personal responsibility for their actions.

But I'm getting off track here by giving you the moral of the story and hints about the ending before I really get the story started. There's a rule about stories: the end has to come after the beginning. If we jumped right to the end, it wouldn't be much of a book, and this book publisher's advertising agency would be left twiddling their thumbs. And you know what they say about idle thumbs.

So just pretend you haven't read any of this.

I know what you're thinking, because you're no dummy. Unlike Hooter Pridley, you're a deep thinker. You're thinking, *Wouldn't it have just been easier not to print this chapter in the first place?* The answer is yes. But I get paid by the word. That last sentence was worth about a hundred dollars.

Anyway, the point is, Hooter Pridley was in love.

That, and there are no mountains in Sterling, Colorado.

chapter Two

The day he fell in love was a Saturday, but beyond that it was a typical day in Hooter Pridley's life. He woke up with Gladys Neidermeyer giving him butterfly kisses. Some mornings she would do other special things that really woke him up and then promptly put him back to sleep again and made him late for work. And Hooter's job was real important. If his customers at Wangdoodle Auto & Truck Parts couldn't get their parts, they couldn't drive, and what would Americans do if they couldn't drive? *Walk?* I don't think so.

Selling cars piece by piece was a lucrative business. You think a car costs a lot new? Huh. Do you have any idea what it costs to build a car piece by piece—even at Wangdoodle prices, which are widely considered to be the most competitive prices around? Me neither. But it's a lot. Hooter Pridley told me.

It's imperative that people get back on the road, driving their cars, smoking cigarettes to make them feel young and vibrant, yapping on their cell phones, and drinking beer that makes them feel like they're in the mountains.

With all of that going on, it's no wonder people get distracted and crash their cars. Car wrecks are good for the medical industry. And even if the medical industry doesn't do a good job of healing you, car wrecks are good for the funeral industry. In general, accidents are good for commerce. And the beautiful thing is, you get to start selling car parts again just to get the wrecks back on the road.

So you can see how Gladys threw a wrench into the system with her morning fellatio and butterfly kisses.

Hooter would be late.

Fewer parts would be sold.

Fewer cars would be driven.

Fewer people would have to be scraped off the interstate.

That would impede commerce. And there are hungry mouths to feed.

Even though her intentions were honorable, Gladys was, if not the cause, a contributing factor to starvation. Every time I see a really skinny person, I think of Gladys Neidermeyer.

But the point is, too much love is bad for the economy. On the other hand, war is good for the economy. Which is why there is so little love and so much war in the world. It's the economy.

So in the beginning, when Hooter dumped Gladys, it seemed like a smart move. Except that Hooter's next move was really dumb. He fell in love with someone else.

A lot of men fell in love with Trixie Foxalot, and most of them didn't even know her name. Not that Trixie Foxalot was her real name. Her agent put her up to that. Maybe I'll tell you what her real name is later on. No sense in telling you now and spoiling it.

Trixie Foxalot was a vision. Hooter saw her for the first time on June first. He was late for work because Gladys and he had enjoyed some afternoon delight, as she liked to call it—though mostly they did it in the mornings. Hooter hustled through the back door and hoped that Peter Wangdoodle, the owner, hadn't beaten him to work. Peter had a vile temper. You never knew what would set him off. He drank expensive scotch because according to the ads, it

5

made you charming. It didn't work, but the purple velvet bags the scotch came in were nice.

But Hooter *had* beaten Peter in to work, so he took a moment to roll the page back on the calendar. It was a free calendar from Red Neck Tools—That Can't Be Broke, or so their motto went. The fact was, they were second-rate tools, and Hooter wasn't inclined to order them. But their calendar was first-rate, and Miss May was a real looker. But May was kaput.

Trixie Foxalot was Miss June. She suggestively held a torque wrench. The chrome gleamed, and she eyed that thing like, like … well, it made you want to go out and buy torque wrenches is what it did. She had on the most fabulous lime green bikini, two sizes too small, so her bounteous bounty overflowed. That was some bikini. Any mortal bikini would have burst from the strain. She wore a blue-and-white striped hat, like railroad engineers used to wear. It was tilted at a saucy angle, like a crown atilt on her cascade of long blonde curls. The idea was, I think, to make her look like she was ready for a full day of torque wrenching.

Hooter stared hard at the picture and the slightly hardened nipples threatening to poke right through that gallant lime green fabric, and that was it. Hooter didn't even realize he was smitten. All he knew was he refused to flip the calendar when July rolled around. When Peter tried to flip it, Hooter stopped him.

"It's July," Peter said.

"I know," said Hooter, "but look at her."

"Fine," Peter said.

From that point on, Peter referred to the calendar with outdoor scenes of places prettier than Sterling, Colorado. This is not to insult the fine people of Sterling. I've been there. It's nice. But they don't have any mountains.

Trixie Foxalot remained on that wall for four months straight. Every month was June. Even then, and only in his subconscious, Hooter was falling in love. Nothing much changed on the surface. He woke up to butterfly kisses and that thing with the handcuffs. He worked. He drank beer that made him feel like he was in the mountains. And he ordered a pile of second-rate torque wrenches from Red Neck Tools.

It wasn't until September that Hooter knew he was in love, and it happened at the Kum and Go. Shirley Baranskey, the night clerk, let him look through the magazines without paying for them, despite the sign that read This Is Not a Library. Which is dumb. Everyone knew it was the Kum and Go. Anyway, Shirley let Hooter break the rules because she had a crush on him. It was ironic that Hooter used his privilege to look at girlie magazines.

At this juncture, I want to point out that Shirley is not a crucial part of the story. See, some people complain when books have too many characters. They get sidetracked while trying to keep tabs on everyone. Some of them even keep charts. And then when they find out that a minor character never appears again, they get irritated because they had worked so hard trying to remember him. Personally, I think they're whiners. I mean, who knows at first who is going to end up being important in your life? It's not like people wear T-shirts that say Important or Not Important, but it would be nice if it worked that way. Then Hooter Pridley would have known right off that Trixie Foxalot was going to change his life forever.

The point is, Shirley Baranskey is not crucial to the plot, though she is very nice.

Hooter paged through the October issue of *Plaything* magazine, though it was only September. That's an old trick that allows a magazine to sit on the shelf for two months without seeming old. But I can't imagine *Plaything* sitting on the shelf for that long without someone buying it. It's a fine publication.

When he got to the centerfold, Hooter was stunned. It was Trixie Foxalot. It said so right there, in her own handwriting.

And Hooter finally got to see those nipples he had been hoping would somehow burst through the lime green bikini on the calendar. They were great. Tiny and erect on those huge tan melons, which made them seem even tinier. For the first time ever in the history of the Sterling, Colorado, Kum and Go, Hooter Pridley actually paid for a *Plaything* magazine.

"Nice night," Shirley said. She perkily handed him the magazine in a brown paper bag so he wouldn't be embarrassed and have people think he was a pervert or a horn dog or something like that.

"Fine," said Hooter, which didn't make much sense.

She counted out the change into Hooter's palm, stroking it gently with each coin. "There you go," Shirley said. She liked him a lot.

"Thanks, Trixie." Hooter said, which was a rude thing for his subconscious to do.

It was a Freudian slip. But don't sweat it. You won't have Shirley Baranskey to kick around any longer. You will never know if she was so crushed that she went home and swallowed fifty sleeping pills or finally pulled the trigger on that .38 snub-nose she kept in the dresser for those lonely nights when she was feeling really low.

You have those whiners to thank for that. In life, people like Shirley Baranskey are important. In books, they are not.

Hey, I didn't make the rules.

chapter Three

Before you get the idea that Hooter Pridley was some sort of lunkhead, out of fairness I ought to point out that it wasn't just Trixie Foxalot's fabulous body and those nipples that made him fall in love. Sure, that's what turned his head in the first place, and for the record, according to official *Plaything* statistics, she was five-feet-eight, one-hundred-twenty pounds, and her measurements were thirty-eight, twenty-six, thirty-four. Her body was a work of art.

Transpose any of those numbers and she would be the dyke matron at the women's prison. Like if she were eight-feet-five, two-hundred-ten pounds, and measured eighty-three, sixty-two, forty-three, that wouldn't be art. Freaky and interesting, but not art. When Hooter saw the numbers come together like that, he knew the divine hand of God was at play.

But it was her brief biography, written in a girlish, loopy scrawl, that made him do what he eventually did. It revealed her soul. Her turn-ons were buff, intellectual men who challenged her. And cuddling by the fireplace at night. She was interested in psychology. One of her turnoffs was men with hair on their backs. Hooter didn't have hair on his back. Clearly, it was destiny.

And she was against war. Hooter's older brother was against war. He had actually been in one. Zack Pridley wasn't much good when he came back from that war, which was fought to teach the rest of the world the American way of life by killing them. You know the one. Zack had both legs and one arm blown off because, believe it or not, some of those dumb bastards out there are against the American way of life. Excuse my language, but it upsets me.

Zack spent his days grateful he still had one hand with which to masturbate. He could hold a beer, a cigarette, and the remote control in that one hand. Zack used to say that he was one of the lucky ones. But like Trixie Foxalot, he was against war, having seen it up close and all. Zack had this theory that maybe if the suits in Washington, DC, could see war up close, or actually sent their own sons to be blown up in them, they wouldn't be so excited about jumping into them. His theory was never considered, because he only had one arm and no legs, and no one took him seriously.

You can see why Trixie Foxalot's enlightened stance against war struck a chord with Hooter.

Furthermore, if she had one wish, it would be world peace. *World peace.* She could have asked the Good Lord to make her right breast just a few centimeters larger, so it was exactly the same size as the other, but in an act of complete selflessness, she chose world peace.

That did it. In that moment Hooter Pridley knew he and Trixie Foxalot would be together someday. He was right about that. You can thank good old Yankee ingenuity and perseverance.

Hooter Pridley's father told him once that if he worked hard enough, there was nothing he could not do, and Hooter never forgot it.

That conversation took place during one of those times when Hooter's dad was unemployed again. Hooter's dad never actually tested his own theory. Say what you will, but those Pridleys had some good theories, which is more than you can say for some folks.

Dear Hooter, Hooter wrote in his diary.

Today they are called journals. It sounds more masculine, even though it is good to be in touch with your feminine side and your inner child. Hooter didn't write *Dear Diary*, because he was slightly dyslexic and it kept coming out *Dear Dairy*, like he was writing to a bunch of milk cows or something. And what would they think of his innermost thoughts? Nothing. They would chew their cud, squirt milk, and moo.

Hooter's dyslexia wasn't so bad that he couldn't spell his own name.

I am in love, Hooter wrote when I was done interrupting him. *Her name is Trixie, and if she could have one wish, it would be world peace. I think she might be on to something. Someday, we'll be together.*

Hooter didn't tell anyone about his obsession. Certainly not Gladys Neidermeyer. She was oblivious. She started each day loving her man unconditionally, with his seed inside her, and then traipsed off to answer phones at Security Life Insurance.

Insurance. Hooter thought it was a racket. You send the company money each month just in case you die. But if you don't die, you lose. The only way to win is to die. Who came up with those rules?

At any rate, Security Life Insurance sounds like a strong, stable company you can trust in case you die.

The other girls at the office were nice. They looked out for Gladys. They kept asking her when Hooter was going to make an honest woman out of her. Because she was living in sin.

"Oh, I love him, and I know he loves me," Gladys always said.

"Then why won't he marry you?" they asked. And then they answered their own rhetorical question in chirpy sing-song voices: "Why buy the cow when the milk's free?"

That's two references to milk cows in one chapter.

I guess when you start philosophizing, cows come up a lot.

For the longest time, Hooter couldn't explain his reluctance to marry.

Once, at a wedding, an old grizzled uncle eyed him skeptically at the free bar. "Why aren't you married?" he asked, as if Hooter were a homosexual, which is what lots of folks think about men who aren't married. Unless they are particularly revolting. Then people understand. Hooter's uncle took a long gulp from his short glass. "You should get married," he said. "Why should *you* be happy?"

Now Hooter understood why he had not proposed to Gladys, despite the fact that he did love her. It wasn't fear of commitment or the conversation with his uncle. He had held off because instinct told him that his true love, Trixie Foxalot, was out there. It all started to come into focus the day he flipped the calendar and made it June.

He searched for a way to tell Gladys. He looked for the right moment. But she was constantly kissing him and making love to him and doing special things for him. Those wouldn't have been good times to bring up something like that.

While he waited for an opportunity to devastate her, he entertained himself by squinting his eyes when they made love, because in the dim morning light Gladys Neidermeyer looked a little like Trixie Foxalot. Her bust was smaller—a lot smaller—and her lips weren't as pouty. And she was a bit wider in the hips. But she had a marvelous butt. That was the one thing about Glady's body that was better than Trixie's. Trixie's butt was sort of flat. If you ever got tired of looking at her breasts, you might notice that.

Hooter sometimes wondered why he was so enamored with asses. They produced vile odors and fecal matter. Yet he adored Gladys's butt. He adored Gladys and making love to her.

After one of those times, Hooter was drifting back to sleep when Gladys said, "I love you, Hooter" and blew out a series of smoke rings.

"I love you, too, Trixie," Hooter said into his pillow.

That became the moment he broke up with Gladys and her excellent buttocks.

chapter **Four**

It took Hooter a good thirty minutes to pick up his things from the front lawn, where Gladys kept heaving them.

"Gladys, let's talk about this," he said.

That was just before she hit him square in the nose with a huge black dildo that he had been unsuccessfully trying to incorporate into their lovemaking sessions.

The postman was walking by at that moment and nearly collapsed from laughter. One does not often see large black penises flying through the air in Sterling, Colorado. Your town may be different.

Hooter rubbed his nose as the postman leaned on the mailbox, choking in mirth.

Gladys glared from the stoop. "On second thought," she sneered, "give that back."

For a sweet girl, she could get pretty mad. But how would you feel if a guy you worshipped and imagined spending your life with suddenly blurted out another woman's name after sex? Then you find out he's leaving you for someone he *doesn't even know*! If anything would make you start throwing huge black penises, that would be it.

You can well imagine Hooter's frame of mind when he arrived at work more than an hour late.

Peter Wangdoodle was a little more than out of sorts too.

He pulled up a good fifteen minutes late. As boss, that was his privilege, he figured.

By then, there was a line of irate customers waiting to buy parts so they could get back on the road and re-crash their vehicles. When you need parts, you need parts, damn it! And when the sign says Open at Eight A.M., it good-goddamn better open at eight! Two of them had broken torque wrenches to return.

After the morning he had had, Peter couldn't imagine things getting worse. But at least no one had thrown a large black penis at him. Peter had awakened with the sort of headache that involves kettledrums in your skull. The folks who sold the scotch in the purple velvet bags had never once shown a kettledrum in their ads. Not even a disclaimer from the surgeon general that read "Overconsumption of this product may lead to someone playing the kettledrums in your head."

Then, with his wife still soundly asleep from an overdose of wine coolers, Peter shakily dressed for work. When he slid his foot into his shoe, it felt funny. When he pulled his foot out, it smelled funny. The cat had crapped in his shoe. Cats will do that if their litter box isn't changed often enough. Just to make a point.

It would be easier if we could talk to the animals so they didn't have to resort to sign language. Not once in his entire career did a cat dump in Dr. Dolittle's shoe. And if one had, I am confident they could have talked it over and come to a peaceful solution. Because they had established a dialogue.

Well, with the kettledrums in his head, the taste of buffalo turds in his mouth, and the cat shit in his shoe, Peter went a little crazy. He scooped up that cat and strangled him then and there. That cat never shat again. But when Peter's breathing settled down from all the excitement, he realized he was in quite a fix. His wife loved that cat. More than him, he figured.

15

Think! his brain said between the banging of kettle-drums. He circled the house with the corpse of the cat still clutched in his hands. The house was messy, because when they started drinking like they had, they agreed that tidying it could wait 'til morning. Then Peter did something I would have never thought of: he grabbed a gnawed chicken leg from a plate on the counter and shoved it down the dead cat's throat. It was pretty big and protruded from the cat's mouth.

The cause of death was obvious: gluttony had killed the cat.

Hooter had no idea that his boss was a cat killer when he walked in that morning. He had no idea that Peter had a kettledrum solo going in his head. Something from Iron Butterfly, I think. Anyway, Hooter was not feeling particu-larly empathetic. He had problems of his own. His nose hurt. So when Peter started in on him about being late, it didn't sit well.

"And two more of those lame-ass torque wrenches came back," Peter said. "You have your head up your ass when you ordered them?"

This was a rhetorical question. It is not possible to have your head up your ass. Not without a great deal of assis-tance. And maybe flexibility exercises.

Hooter handled the barrage pretty well. He had been through worse. Not as bad as that cat, mind you, but plenty bad. But he noticed that whenever Peter got close to him to yell, he smelled like cat crap. He just wanted Peter to stop hollering and stinking so he could think about his own problems.

Peter turned and began stomping down the parts aisle in the back, keeping time with the drum in his head. Then he spotted Trixie Foxalot and her subpar torque wrenches. That set him off again. He reached up to turn the calendar to September.

"Don't!" Hooter said.

"If I see one more freakin' torque wrench today, I am going to come unglued," Peter said. "And I'm tired of looking at this stupid whore too!"

Whore, he had called her. That did it. Hooter popped him one right in the nose.

Now both of their noses were hurting. Peter glared at Hooter. He spat a bloody hunk of goo right on Trixie Foxalot's torque wrench. Then he leveled Hooter with a roundhouse right that sent him rolling over the counter.

For an older, hungover guy, Peter was no slouch. He was feeling pretty good about himself, studying his surprisingly potent right fist, when Hooter tackled him. They crashed into an end cap of STP Oil Treatment, which Andy Granatelli used to endorse.

Pay no mind to Andy Granatelli. He is not a crucial plot element. But he was right about STP being a superior lubricant, judging from the way Hooter and Peter slipped around in the stuff that leaked out of the cans.

They would stand, their legs would windmill about, and then they would fall down without either having struck the other. To the customers walking in, it looked like some crazy new dance kids would do. Eventually Hooter and Peter stopped trying to hit each other and just concentrated on standing. By that time, the customers were breaking it up anyway.

"You're fired!" Peter told Hooter. He snatched Trixie Foxalot from the wall and flung her at Hooter. "Take your stupid calendar, too!" he yelled.

Hooter said a bunch of stuff I would be embarrassed to repeat. And that's saying something.

Peter watched as Hooter stormed out, spreading his arms like wings to knock items off shelves all the way to the front door. Then Peter turned to a customer and said, "What can I do for you?"

"Got a busted torque wrench," the man said.

* * *

Dear Hooter, Hooter wrote into his journal after he had sat and stared at the windshield for hours and contemplated the happenings of the day. *I quit my job today. I also broke up with Gladys. I needed a change. Today is a new beginning. I have decided to drive to Los Angeles to meet Trixie Foxalot and fulfill our destiny together.*

He turned the switch on the ignition, and the 426 in his 1970 Plymouth Barracuda growled. He was going to head a couple miles out of town to the truck stop to gas up, even though it was only a few blocks to the Kum and Go, the reason being I didn't want him to take a chance of bumping into Shirley Baranskey and upsetting the whiners who are too easily distracted by extraneous characters in novels.

Well, wouldn't you know, Hooter was almost to the exit when the engine coughed and went silent. He was out of gas. The gas gauge didn't work. It always indicated a quarter tank, which goes to show that you can't believe everything you read.

Hooter retrieved the small red gas can he kept in the trunk. It was wedged among all his belongings, including the big black dildo. He had kept it out of spite after Gladys threw a whole armload of his underwear into the branches of the elm tree in the front yard so the postman could see all the faded brown streaks and other things in his shorts a guy doesn't want anyone to see.

Well, Hooter walked half a block to the Kum and Go, and who do you suppose he ran into? Shirley Baranskey.

Hey, don't blame me. The man needed gas.

It was Shirley's first day back on the job after having her stomach pumped, so cut her a little slack, would you?

"Ran out of gas, huh?" she asked Hooter. She couldn't look him in the eye, because then she thought he might see how much she liked him. Adored, really. And it was all futile, wasn't it?

"Yeah," Hooter said, and he was glad to be talking to someone who wasn't yelling at him. "Say, did you change your hair? Looks nice."

Shirley beamed. She noticed Hooter's nose was swollen, but she didn't want to ask about anything that would break the spell of the moment. " ... and forty-five," she said, as she counted out his change, stroking his palm with each coin. "Thanks, Hooter."

Hooter gave her his nicest smile. "See you, Trixie," he said.

chapter Five

Hooter was ten miles east of Fort Morgan when a sense of insecurity overtook him. He realized he had never been this alone. In his mind he kept seeing reruns of Gladys Neidermeyer slamming the door. He wished she would come back out and throw more of his underwear into the tree.

In that desperately lonely moment, he saw a winsome figure on the shoulder of the road. It was Andy Granatelli.

No, no! My mistake. Turns out, it was Shawnika Hakim. But at a distance she looked a little like Andy Granatelli. When the Barracuda rumbled to a stop, Hooter saw another body stand up. It was Tyrone X. He had been sitting, hidden below the approach, because while many drivers will stop for an attractive young woman, not many had ever stopped for Tyrone. Many drivers have a hitchhiker fantasy. Most do not involve a large black man with dreadlocks.

They both had dreadlocks. He seemed nice enough, so Hooter let Tyrone into the car too. He rode shotgun. Shawnika hopped in the back. Upon further review, she looked a bit like Diana Ross, but she was missing a tooth. She and Tyrone were going to Denver because there were mountains there, and because they were down to their last spliff and Tyrone knew a guy on East Colfax with a few pounds of good herb. Tyrone and Shawnika were Rastafarians—God told them to smoke marijuana. You know, if you think about it, God is kind of a smart aleck. He tells some folks to smoke weed and then he tells other folks to arrest them. It makes you wonder. What if there are entire classrooms of Gods waiting for assignment? Maybe we got the class clown.

Anyway, Hooter learned Tyrone had been a Pittsburgh steelworker with a union job until he was fired. It seems management wanted him to stop smoking marijuana, even though he was under strict orders from God.

Hooter thought he and Tyrone had a lot in common. They both had lost their jobs because of their religion. Tyrone had been worshipping marijuana; Hooter had been worshipping Trixie Foxalot. He didn't discuss that observation with Tyrone because lots of people don't like to discuss religion with complete strangers.

As Tyrone talked, Hooter adjusted his mirror so he could look at Shawnika. When Tyrone turned to include her in the conversation, she smiled in that practiced way actresses do in public. But Hooter noticed her eyes weren't smiling along with her mouth, and when Tyrone looked away, she looked almost mournful.

Hooter found that sad look incredibly attractive. Some guys are like that. They are suckers for troubled, beautiful women. They want to rescue them and make them happy. That's impossible, of course. Some people aren't happy unless they're miserable. It's a conundrum.

Gladys Neidermeyer never needed rescuing. She smiled all the time. Plus, she was a world-class boinker. Sometimes I wonder, *What was Hooter thinking?*, but that's only because I know how things turn out. If you study any photo of Trixie Foxalot, you will notice that her eyes aren't smiling. But Hooter didn't see that. Love is blind.

Tyrone X really seemed to love Shawnika, despite her missing tooth. In a Jamaican accent that faded in and out, Tyrone told about the day "I blessed my eyes on Shawnika," who was serving grits at Petunia's in the French Quarter at the time. *Blessed my eyes. What a poetic way of saying he fell in love*, Hooter thought.

Eventually the conversation turned to their discontents. That's typical. People will complain about things that are wrong in their lives but hardly even acknowledge the things that are right. Take Tyrone, for instance. He had a beautiful woman at his side. He had enough cash for a bag of killer weed. And he had his health. Still, he got on a rant about The Man.

He had an uncle who was a Black Panther until The Man tossed him in prison. Now he was Fat LeRoy's bitch in Attica. It was The Man's fault that Tyrone didn't have his union job. The Man ate cake and left crumbs for the poor.

Hooter didn't know who The Man was exactly, but he got pretty riled up too. He started punctuating Tyrone's statements about revolution with things he thought Tyrone would like to hear. Things like "Right on!" "Power to the people!" and "Word up!" After a while, though, Hooter began to run out of fresh responses to Tyrone's revolutionary talk, and he shouted things like "Semper fi" and finally, "You go, girl!"

That last one brought an uncomfortable silence to the car as Tyrone glared at Hooter, trying to decide if he was disrespecting him.

In the ominous silence, Hooter stared at the road. He could feel Tyrone's eyes on him. Finally Hooter blurted out in desperation, "Screw The Man!"

Tyrone eased back into his leather seat, pursed his lips, and nodded slightly. "Screw The Man!" he said.

"Screw The Man." Hooter said again.

"Screw … The … Man!" Tyrone agreed.

The Man was so screwed.

Shawnika squirmed in the backseat. She had seen Tyrone like this. She knew it was a momentary truce. In time, things would fester, and Tyrone would start to put two and two together. The Man was white, and Hooter was white. Inevitably, Tyrone would conclude that Hooter was The Man.

Heck, for a split second, I thought Shawnika was Andy Granatelli, so you can see how those things can happen. The world is filled with cases of mistaken identity. *Say, don't I know you from someplace?*

To mellow the situation, Shawnika produced their last joint. She carried the marijuana and the money because Tyrone was constantly being frisked. The cops never touched Shawnika, because she was pretty and looked a bit vulnerable. That's like cop kryptonite.

So they drove and smoked. Hooter had never before smoked marijuana, but because it was endorsed by God, he didn't see any harm in it. But the more he smoked, the faster the world around him seemed to be moving, and the less he could handle it. Pretty soon he was chugging along at forty miles per hour in his Barracuda, which was a complete waste of horsepower.

A few miles from Denver, as Hooter looked into his mirror to admire Shawnika, he noticed the flash of red and blue lights behind his car. It was The Man. Panicked, Hooter looked down at the nub of the joint in the ashtray.

Tyrone picked it up, popped it into his mouth, and swallowed it. "Relax, mon," he said. "We're clean."

The highway patrolman leaned into Hooter's window. Hooter had his license and registration ready.

"Car problems?" the patrolman asked, eyeing the other passengers.

Uh ... ," said Hooter.

"Because you were only going thirty-eight miles per hour. Forty-five's the minimum on the interstate."

"Yeah. Yeah. Clogged gas line, I think," Hooter said. "It's cleared up now."

The officer asked for Tyrone and Shawnika's identification and asked them to remain in the vehicle while he escorted Hooter to the patrol car to write him a ticket for going too slow on the interstate in a Barracuda with five hundred horsepower.

The numbers were punched into the computer. Hooter's record was clean. But the patrolman noted that Hooter had once been clocked going a hundred miles faster than he was driving today. There were no outstanding warrants on Shawnika or Tyrone, but the patrolman concluded from Tyrone's rap sheet that he was certainly a faithful Rastafarian. When God said, "Smoke," he smoked.

"Oswald," the officer said to Hooter, because that was his given name, "I believe I detected the odor of marijuana in your vehicle."

That wasn't exactly the truth. But Tyrone's record of worshipping God made the officer conclude that he must have smelled *something*. He was telling a little white lie to himself. He looked into Hooter's glassy eyes. "You high?"

Hooter was becoming more depressed by the second. "No," he lied.

"You mind if I take a look in your vehicle then?"

The patrolman went on to explain that Hooter didn't *have* to allow a search at that moment. He *could* wait until a warrant was procured, and who knows how long *that* would take. And then they would search the car anyway.

As Hooter considered his options, Shawnika was busy trying to calm Tyrone, whose incendiary rants against The Man were escalating.

Hooter sighed. "Go ahead. We're clean."

The unlikely trio stood on the shoulder of the road in the September dusk. Tyrone X continued to mutter unkind things as the officer poked about in the immaculate machine. Shawnika smiled nervously, and Hooter absently wondered what had happened to her tooth.

After searching under the seats, the officer sifted through Hooter's worldly possessions in the trunk. It was becoming clear that if there was anything to be found, it wouldn't be much. Besides, his shift was almost over. There would be paperwork.

With two fingers, he lifted the underwear Hooter had managed to retrieve from the tree. The patrolman didn't ask about the bits of leaves and branches in the underwear. But he couldn't help himself. He had to know one thing. "What's the deal with the big black dildo?"

At this, Tyrone flew into a rage. Because he thought the officer was referring to *him*. And he began spouting things far more pointed than "Screw The Man." A good deal of anatomy was covered in the rant, with a confusing array of unlikely interactions between the parts, before Tyrone segued into the officer's lineage and accused him of having carnal relations with his mother. But not in those words exactly.

That is how Tyrone came to spend his first night in Denver in jail.

He would be in court at nine the next morning, the officer advised Shawnika.

The patrolman drove off with Tyrone X staring forlornly out the back window. There was an uncomfortable silence between the unarrested. Hooter stared at his shoes. Suddenly being alone with a woman he had been fantasizing about made him feel a little dirty.

"Do you want me to drop you off someplace?" he asked Shawnika finally. "Don't know nobody here," Shawnika said with a voice of pure, sweet clover honey, which any beekeeper will tell you is the champagne of all honey.

They drove in silence for a while. Hooter was disappointed that it was too dark to get a good look at the mountains.

"I guess maybe I'll get a room," Shawnika said. "What are you going to do?"

"Probably keep driving to the mountains. Sleep in the car." Hooter wanted to wake up in the mountains and see them in the spectacular morning light. It would be just like a beer commercial.

Shawnika got a room for twenty-six dollars on North Federal. Hooter carried her backpack to her room, because he was a gentleman and he was thinking about asking her what had happened to her tooth—it would be his last chance—but decided that that wouldn't be polite.

"Well, good night," he said. "Sorry about how things went today."

She touched his wrist. "Stay. I don't want to be alone. Not tonight."

It was a line from an old movie she had seen, and she delivered it beautifully. Between you and me, she was a better actress than Trixie Foxalot ever was.

chapter Six

Shawnika felt naughty. God, did she feel naughty. And all the repressed anger she had ever felt toward Tyrone escaped as she pistoned down violently upon Hooter. Shawnika's breasts were cupped in his hands, and when Hooter pinched her ebony nipples hard, she orgasmed. That fascinated him. She moaned and arched her back in the low glow of the streetlights streaming in through the curtains. She scratched him and bit his chest. When she sensed him flagging, her low, honeyed moan urged him on.

Several times throughout the night, he tried to get some sleep, but Shawnika kept waking him. Not that Hooter protested much. Her lithe, supple body was warm, and the firm mounds of flesh that formed her buttocks, magnificent. She was much better in bed than Andy Granatelli would have been. We can make that assumption.

When she was finally satiated, Shawnika wiggled her rear into Hooter's groin. She wanted to be ready if he managed another resurrection. *His penis is larger than Tyrone's*, she thought with perverse satisfaction. That was the real root of Tyrone's anger. He thought all large black men should have large black wangs. Heck, he was a jackhammer in bed, so Shawnika never minded that he was a bit small. Or so she said. But it bothered Tyrone that there were millions of white guys out there with larger penises than his. That was his paranoid assumption, anyway. It's not like he was out there measuring. That sort of thing is best left to medical-research professionals. The last thing we need in this country are rank amateurs running around with yardsticks asking guys to whip it out.

While Shawnika's breasts rose and fell hypnotically with each sleeping breath, Hooter stared at them. Now, when he really needed to sleep, he could not. In the last twenty-four hours, he had been hit in the nose with a dildo and had danced aggressively in a pool of STP with his cat-killer boss. He had been fired, arrested for driving too slow in a really fast car, worshipped God by smoking pot, and made love to a woman who looked like Diana Ross with dental issues. That will get the wheels turning.

Hooter sighed and clicked the remote control. He rolled through the channels, stopping for a moment on a twenty-four-hour movie channel out of Burbank. *The Flight of the Phoenix* was playing. He loved that movie. Jimmy Stewart had just discovered Ernest Borgnine dead in the desert when they cut to a commercial.

It was bedlam.

Crazy Sheldon was screaming about the lowest prices ever. Pictures of electronics and Sheldon's excited, flushed face flashed on the screen. No one had ever seen such low prices! *He's probably losing money on every sale,* Hooter thought. *But maybe Sheldon isn't crazy,* Hooter mused as he drifted off to a blessed slumber. *Perhaps Sheldon just takes joy in bringing discount electronics to the needy. That's not how the authorities saw it, though.*

Hooter's eyes narrowed, but were jolted open by the racket Sheldon made as a uniformed policeman dragged him from the store in a straitjacket. It reminded Hooter of the way Tyrone had been dragged to the patrol car.

Sheldon kept shouting out the bargains as he was lurched along. You could get a boom box for twenty-five dollars. A nineteen-inch color television for only eighty-nine dollars. Cable ready, even.

Give him credit. Sheldon was motivated to turn capitalism on its ear, but that's not what impressed Hooter the most. It was the huge-breasted nurse attempting to restrain Sheldon. She cushioned his deranged head in her bosom and smiled comfortingly at the camera to let viewers know the poor man was in good hands.

It was Trixie Foxalot, and in that instant Hooter wished *he* were Crazy Sheldon.

chapter Seven

The dildo was entered as evidence.

When they finished explaining everything to the judge and a contrite Tyrone X apologized to The Man, he was released. In light of the misunderstanding, the judge imposed a suspended sentence, but ordered Tyrone to pay court costs of seventy-nine dollars.

Hooter was too embarrassed to ask for the return of the evidence. There had been enough hilarity in the courtroom. The paunchy bailiff had laughed so hard, he began wheezing, releasing fine droplets of spittle into the air and drizzling snot from his nose. If Hooter had analyzed his attachment to the dildo, he would have realized he had kept it because it reminded him of Gladys Neidermeyer. In that regard, it was an unusual keepsake. Most folks just keep a photo in their wallet and call it good.

True, some rock bands have gone so far as to name themselves after a famous dildo, but as far as I'm concerned, the less said about dildos (or is it dildi?), the better. I forget exactly which band that was. AC/DC? Maybe it was Weezer.

After driving in silence for an interminable twenty minutes, Hooter dropped Tyrone and Shawnika on East Colfax. A sullen Tyrone didn't even say thank you. Instinct told him *something* had happened between Hooter and Shawnika, and that was killing him. He began to meander away, but Shawnika paused long enough to lean into the window and whisper a quiet good-bye. She liked him. Hooter was lucky that way, with women of the opposite sex. With the scent of her minty breath still hanging in the air, Hooter inhaled deeply and watched Tyrone and Shawnika grow smaller in his mirror. Tyrone seemed animated. Then he decked Shawnika, and Hooter understood about the tooth.

Alone again, Hooter was unsettled, and he knew what it was. Guilt. He had cheated on Trixie Foxalot before he had even met her. It's hard to get much lower than that.

Dear Hooter, he wrote in his journal as he munched a breakfast burrito in the parking lot of a fast-food restaurant. *I now know how to find my one true love, Trixie Foxalot. I will ask Crazy Sheldon. I said good-bye to Tyrone and Shawnika this morning. Something seems to have come between them. I guess we all have our problems. Love is a battlefield.*

When he was done, he unfolded and studied the increasingly tattered centerfold of Trixie Foxalot. Her breasts were amazing. They did not sag. Not one little bit. It was as if some antigravity device was propping them up. One gleaming fingernail was poised beneath the elastic of her blue lace panties. Maybe she had an itch.

Hooter read her biography again. He tried to memorize everything about her. The fact that she was interested in psychology concerned him, though. Hooter didn't know beans about psychology, and he didn't want to blow it when he finally found his one true love. He didn't have time for college courses, so he settled for a bookstore. Perhaps he could learn enough psychology to impress Trixie Foxalot. Or at least enough to get by.

"Are you a Freudian or a Jungian?" the clerk asked at the bookstore.

"Lutheran," Hooter said.

He bought books by Freud *and* Jung, just to be on the safe side.

31

Hooter was never one for studies, but in high school his grades were decent, if unspectacular. In trade school, though, where he learned about the mysteries of the combustion engine, he was near the top of the class. Now he was majoring in Trixie Foxalot.

He drove into the mountains for the first time in years—to the top of Mount Evans, 14,264 feet high. It had been an uncommonly warm and dry autumn. He was grateful the road remained clear of snow. But it was cold at that altitude. The wind knifed between the mountain peaks.

He spent two days on the mountain reading Freud and Jung. In the daylight, the sun warmed him enough so he could lean against a tire and read. At night, he ran the engine every couple hours and read beneath the dome light.

Freud seemed to think that every psychosis had something to do with sex and phallic symbols. All Hooter knew about phalli was that they could lead to arrest. Freud gave Hooter a headache, though part of it might have been from the altitude. Jung, on the other hand, was a mystic who believed in a collective unconscious and the symbolism of dreams. They were both nutty, Hooter decided, but Jung was a more pleasant kind of crazy.

Maybe there is some symbolism to Hooter going to a mountaintop to receive the word of Freud. Like Moses on Mount Sinai chiseling out dictation from God. The difference is, Moses was busy freeing his people. The first oppressed man Hooter met on the road had been jailed. That's where the similarity ends.

Another thing: If you plopped the word of Sigmund Freud down on stone tablets in a courthouse, no one would even notice. The Ten Commandments—that's another thing. There would be protests and endless public meetings. People argue over separation of church and state all the time. There's no law mandating separation of *intellectuals* and state.

They do it anyway, though.

Hooter didn't much go in for religion, though his mother made him go to church "as long as he was under her roof and his feet were under her table." Church was a lot like cod liver oil to Hooter. After his mother wasn't around to make him take it, he didn't. Not that Hooter had anything against God. He just didn't believe preachers had any better fix on God than anyone else. Especially the ones on television who claimed to know in specific detail what God wanted.

God was *saddened* by homosexuality. God liked classy architecture, so he ordered preachers to build crystal cathedrals and such. Just like he told Noah to build the ark. Except nobody measures in cubits anymore, and you can't bring a pair of giraffes into church. God was a Republican, despite the fact that he sent his only son into Jerusalem on a donkey. God shalt throw you a few curveballs along the way.

Apparently, God had a cash-flow problem, because television evangelists were always asking Hooter's mother to mail them money. Did you ever wonder why God is always broke? It's simple. As noted previously, war is good for the economy, but God is determined to spread love, which is only good for the economy on Valentine's Day. You'd think God would wise up and get with the program.

The television preachers would pass the donations they received from folks like Hooter's mother on to God, of course. Pinky promise. But the really cool thing about it—so the preachers said—was that God would give the money back *tenfold*. Hooter's mother viewed it as an investment strategy.

But Hooter's mom never hit the mother lode. She just kept sending some guy in a white suit and big hair half her Social Security check each month. She was as faithful as any little old lady at a nickel slot machine. Her money helped pay for hairstylists and hair spray. I always wondered why preachers wouldn't want to emulate Jesus, who had hippie hair. Instead, the evangelists all wanted to look like Conway Twitty.

Here's the funny part. While her faith in God never wavered, Hooter's mother never believed in Social Security. She watched the news, and every four years important-looking men in nice suits accused each other of trying to bankrupt Social Security. So she had no faith in Social Security being there month to month. Yet those checks came like clockwork.

She never got a check from God. She concluded it was because she was a wretched sinner, and she felt guilty about that. Guilty enough to switch denominations from Lutheran to Catholic, a philosophy more heavily steeped in guilt. I'm not criticizing. Everyone knows that without guilt, there would be too much fun. It would be anarchy.

Hooter's mother confessed her sins every week to a man who had a thing for altar boys. Some weeks she couldn't think of any sinning she had done, so she made something up, and after a while it got so she couldn't remember which sins were real and which were not. It doesn't matter, though. She was forgiven.

That sort of thing is why Carl Jung and Sigmund Freud were invented—to straighten out all the folks confused by religion. That's the way Hooter had it figured, anyway. If this book bursts into flame as you are reading it, you will know he was wrong. Or else your house is on fire.

chapter **Eight**

West of Colorado lies the great state of Utah. So when Hooter descended from the mountains with the theories of Freud and Jung rattling about in his mind, that was the next stop.

Lots of people think that the first thing that will happen to them when they get to Utah is that they're going to run into a Mormon family consisting of one man and five wives. Just because that's what happened to Hooter Pridley is no reason for you to expect such a thing. Polygamy is no longer what God wants in Utah; it's what he *used* to want. But he changed his mind. In the Old Testament he sent down plagues, floods, and angels of death and turned even fairly nice people into pillars of salt. But in the New Testament he became a more merciful god, a god of love. God went soft.

That's the way Wayne Noodler and all five Mrs. Noodlers saw it. God had gone soft. At least the Mormon church had. If Wayne could have swung it, he would have had forty wives, because he was a very religious man, and even if God had compromised his values, he hadn't. Wayne worked odd jobs and tapped a dwindling inheritance to keep his five wives and eleven children in a row of bleak trailer houses.

When they advertise trailer houses, they call them mobile homes because it sounds more prestigious. As if you might find the Rockefellers living in one. The truth is, mobile homes aren't all that mobile. They get plopped down, hoses and wires get run into them, and they stand there, mired in the dirt, until the next tornado rolls through. At that point, they become mobile again.

So far, God had not seen fit to turn Wayne Noodler's mobile homes into airplanes, and Wayne took it as a sign that he was on a righteous path. If God had kicked in a few extra shillings each month, that would have been nice too.

Four days after he began his quest to find Trixie Foxalot, Hooter Pridley met Wayne Noodler, mayor, maintenance man, and sultan of Noodler's Bluff. The town consisted of the aforementioned mobile homes and a tin shack with a pair of two-hundred-fifty-gallon gas tanks beside it. Inside the spartan shack, travelers could buy two-dollar candy bars and five-dollar gas. It was a princely sum for eighty-five octane. It was also fifty-six miles to the next town. Hooter couldn't risk it with his busted gas gauge, especially after motoring up and down Utah's peaks and valleys. He couldn't begin to guess what sort of mileage his Barracuda was getting. He decided to get just enough gas to get him to the next town, Upchuck, Utah.

Now that is an interesting name for a town, Hooter thought. Wayne couldn't tell Hooter how Upchuck got its name. He *could* tell him how Noodler's Bluff got its name: because he named it. He thought it sounded like some place John Wayne would hang out. He loved the Duke, despite the fact that the Duke was not a Mormon. A lot of Hollywood stars are Scientologists, which is a whole other ball of wax, Wayne explained. They believe in a dead science fiction writer.

"Probably no weirder than worshipping a carpenter," Hooter said after listening politely.

"You've got a point," Wayne said.

"I'll take five gallons," Hooter said.

"No can do," said Wayne. "She's bone dry. But the bulk driver will be here later today. Tomorrow at the latest."

He was stranded. Hmm ... Hooter pondered his dilemma. All the Pridleys were ponderers. There was a preponderance of ponderers in that family. His cousin Dion, who was a Pridley on his father's side, even wrote a song about it. The record company didn't think a song about ponderers would sell, though. They equated pondering with procrastinating. Really, though, pondering is just sitting around until an idea comes to you. You can call it procrastinating, but it is an unappreciated science, as far as Hooter was concerned.

At any rate, Dion's record company thought a song about a wanderer sounded better. You want songs about people who appear to be doing something. Turns out, the record company was right. Take Ricky Nelson, for instance. He changed everything about one of his songs to make it a hit. When he started out with *Pondering Man*, the verses were something like:

> *I'm a pondering man,*
> *Sitting on my ass,*
> *I'm a pondering man,*
> *Wish someone'd mow my grass.*

But once the record company got old Ricky up and moving, he was meeting pretty Polynesian babies, sweet fräuleins, and little señoritas all over the place. The rest is history. According to the song, Ricky Nelson never met a Mormon girl, like Hooter did. How could Hooter help it, being stranded in a town where the wives outnumber the husbands five to one?

First there was Ernestine Noodler, who had a clubfoot. She was toting buckets of water from a large steel tank to each trailer, splashing with each limp.

"Well went dry last week," Wayne explained. "Had to improvise. For drinking only. No flushing. Got an outhouse out back if you need it."

And there was Sandra, Twyla, Brenda, and Gretchen.

Sandra had a hooknose and a goiter.

Twyla had immense, flapping ears and, ironically, was hard of hearing.

As previously documented, love is blind. So was Brenda.

Gretchen was a hunchback. She was the newest Noodler. She and Wayne had only been married since June. She had two children from a previous marriage, Marcie and Matilda.

Marcie and Matilda wore white pasty makeup and dressed in black with lots of silver buckles and studs. They were pierced pretty much everywhere. Even Custer didn't get it that bad. Marcie and Matilda were Goths, which means that they dressed as if they lived in the Middle Ages, a time well known for its dreariness and hopelessness. Say you're a time traveler. The Middle Ages is not where you want to go to party. The sixties were good, though.

Anyway, Marcie and Matilda walked around looking bored and hopeless. Teenagers haven't changed much since the Middle Ages. The twins were seventeen. Wayne Noodler planned to marry them when they turned eighteen—which was tomorrow. Wayne had it in his head that marrying twins would somehow be more legal if he waited until they were eighteen.

"You could be a witness," Wayne offered hopefully.

Hooter had already been a witness in a Denver courtroom and had been forced to explain to a packed house exactly why he kept a dildo next to the tire iron in his trunk. He had come to the conclusion that witnessing wasn't his thing.

"Wouldn't I have to be a Mormon to make it official?" Hooter asked in an effort to weasel out of it.

"We could always convert you," Wayne said.

Hooter thought about it. There were advantages. He imagined his life with Trixie Foxalot. Sure, she was more woman than any man needed, but if he had the option, stepping next door to have at it with Shawnika Hakim or even Gladys Neidermeyer, well, that was something to consider. He started to imagine marrying Marcie and Matilda too. Although they weren't cheerful, he found them alluring. They had not inherited their mother's hump.

Hooter had a thing for Goths long before Gothing became the thing to do. Once his mother caught him masturbating to *The Munsters*—Lily Munster, specifically. The incident irreparably damaged Hooter's relationship with his God-fearing mother. She thought anyone who could spank the monkey to *The Munsters* must be some kind of sicko. Hooter was also quite fond of *The Addams Family*. And Elvira. Oh, God, Elvira.

Hooter was jostled away from his pondering when he noticed a dust cloud in the distance.

Wayne saw it too. "Must be the bulk truck," Wayne said. "I guess you'll be on your way in no time flat."

chapter Nine

Wayne Noodler was wrong. It wasn't the bulk truck rumbling down the road to replenish the gas tanks at Noodler's One Stop. It was One-Eyed Jack Lipensky from Upchuck, the best and only dowser in three counties.

You might think from his name that One-Eyed Jack was missing an eye. In actuality, he was missing his left arm. Somebody in Upchuck came up with the ironic idea to call him One-Eyed Jack. People there thought it was hilarious.

Jack lost the arm in the worst car wreck folks around there had seen in years. It took out six Mormons, two Catholics, and an atheist. Jack was the only survivor. He was Methodist. Draw your own conclusions.

The handicap threw off Jack's dowsing. Most dowsers use two hands to wave a tree branch or a wire over the ground until some mysterious force pulls it down.

Jack took up drinking after the accident, out of guilt, though he wasn't even driving when it happened. Every so often, Jack would drink too much and some mysterious force would pull him down too. Between the drinking and the missing arm, Jack's dowsing wasn't what it used to be. Truly, there's nothing sadder than a washed-up one-armed dowser.

These days, Jack didn't often find what he was looking for. Once, when the cops hired him to look for the body of a murder victim, Jack led them to the bones of an armadillo.

No arrests were made in what appeared to be a hit and run. He should have gotten more credit for the find—it was the first armadillo ever documented as far north as Utah. Another time, some guy from back East hired him to help find a lost gold mine his uncle told him about. Jack led him to a tail fin from a 1957 Chevy.

After a while, Jack started drawing crowds when word got out that he was dowsing. It was always a real hoot to see what he would find. That he arrived that day without being followed was a wonder.

Now Wayne Noodler didn't really expect Jack to find the right spot to dig a well. He hadn't even planned to call Jack, but Jack got wind of Wayne's predicament and offered his services.

"If I don't find any water, you don't have to pay me," he said.

That was the standard agreement, which is why Jack was on welfare.

There wasn't much call for drunken one-armed dowsers. But Jack knew there was a good chance Wayne would give him a couple bottles of wine from his stash under the counter at Noodler's One Stop even if Jack didn't find water. You couldn't get wine from most Mormons. Wayne wasn't a strict Mormon in that regard. He had helped Jack out a time or two before.

One-Eyed Jack Lipensky dowsed all afternoon. A throng of Noodlers followed along behind. Even the Goths came out. But they seemed just as interested in watching Hooter. Jack found a fence post, the corpse of a coyote, a decent piece of turquoise, and an old Burma Shave sign that said "Doesn't kiss you like she useter? Perhaps she's seen a smoother rooster! Burma Shave."

Jack played out at about seven P.M. and decided to stay the night so he could get an early start. Besides, he was low on gas, he said. Wayne said fine. Jack could bunk with Twyla, the deaf one with the big ears.

"On the couch, of course," Wayne added. "Maybe in the morning when I marry the twins, you can be a witness."

"Sure," Jack said. He waited around for a few moments just in case Wayne might be inclined to slip him a bottle.

But Wayne knew Jack's dowsing skills would disintegrate completely if he was hungover. He would serve no wino before his time.

"Don't look like the bulk truck is coming," Wayne told Hooter. The only other spare bed was a fold-out couch in Sandra's trailer. She was the one with the nose. "You can sleep there," Wayne offered.

"Thanks," Hooter said, "but I'm getting kind of used to sleeping in the car."

"Suit yourself," Wayne said, and off he went to sleep with Brenda, the blind one.

Wayne treasured his evenings with Brenda because she was childless, and one night without having to tuck in kids and deal with the endless demands for water and goodnight kisses was a relief. Sleeping in Brenda's trailer was not without its challenges, though. It was cluttered. Navigation was further complicated because the ever-frugal Wayne never replaced the lightbulbs when they burned out in her trailer. Brenda never minded. Sacrifices must be made to provide for five wives and eleven kids. Tomorrow it would be seven wives and nine children. That's a genealogy you wouldn't want to do.

There were complications beyond the family tree. Wayne would have to get another trailer for the twins. He had enough from his waning inheritance to last another year or so. At that point, he would have to put most of his wives back on the street. He had told no one that, of course. He would keep the twins. He had already decided that. He didn't have enough money to keep them all. To do that would require a miracle.

chapter Ten

It was midnight, and Hooter had his eyes closed when he heard a tapping that didn't keep time with the music of Prince Albert the Dogman, an obscure bluesman Hooter had never heard of before. The tapping became more persistent as the song drifted away on the wings of a distant blues station that didn't flap quite far enough.

Tap. Tap. Tap.

Hooter slowly emerged from his dreams as he slept in the backseat. He turned his face to the side window. *Jesus!* A ghostly white face peered in, and then another. It was the Goths.

"Open up," Marcie said, her voice muted by the glass.

She was the one with a pierced lip and Chinese lettering on the back of her neck.

Hooter rolled down the window.

Matilda held a bottle of wine in each hand. "Yeah, let us in. It's cold out here."

The metal bar through her nose gave her voice an adenoidal quality. As she leaned in, her modest, unrestrained breasts were outlined by her white cotton nightshirt. Marcie wore one too.

Hooter scanned the line of trailers for any sign of movement. No noise. No lights. He opened the door, and they scrambled in beside him. "What gives?" he asked.

"Let's party," Matilda said. She took a swig and purposely dribbled enough down her chin to soak one breast. Through the outline of the cotton, Hooter could see a metal ring looped through the nipple.

"Uh, look ... ," Hooter said. His heart rate was up.

"We're at the age of consent," Marcie said, leaning into Hooter from the other side. "We've been eighteen for five minutes now."

She laughed a little-girl laugh that reminded him of champagne glasses breaking. That freaked Hooter out. A happy Goth is somehow weirder than a despondent Goth.

"Oh, Jesus," Hooter said. He snatched a bottle from Matilda and gulped a third of it. "What do you want?"

But with Marcie's black fingernails brushing gently along the swelling outline of his crotch, he was beginning to understand. With a trembling hand, he cupped Matilda's wet breast. He jerked his hand away and looked again for any sign of motion in the trailers. Then, a burst of conscience: he remembered Trixie Foxalot and the beautiful soul inside that magnificent body and her quest for world peace. He vowed not to cheat on her again. "I can't do this," Hooter said.

You have to give him credit. He had more willpower than I would have had.

"Do what?" Matilda asked in that nasal voice as she unbuttoned her gown so Hooter could see the soft slope of her breasts. She pulled his trembling hand to them.

Hooter felt Marcie slide his zipper down.

"There's just one thing," Matilda said.

Hooter moaned.

"Take us with you tomorrow."

Hooter jerked upright. "Wha ... Wha ... Why?"

"We can't marry Wayne," Marcie said. "I couldn't bear it."

"You're against polygamy?" Hooter asked.

Marcie laughed her glass-tinkling laugh. "Does it look like we have a problem with sharing a man?"

"But Wayne is creepy looking," Matilda explained. "And old. He weirds me out."

"Take us with you—at least to Nevada," Marcie said, pulling her gown over her head. She was pierced *down there*. She maneuvered a pale breast to Hooter's mouth. "Deal?"

"Mgfph," Hooter said.

• • •

The day Wayne Noodler's miracle came, he awakened early, about four A.M. He checked the alarm and burrowed under the covers next to Brenda for a few more hours of sleep. But what was that sound? At first he thought it was the contraction of the tin on the trailer, but it was rhythmic and barely audible. He leaned toward the window and saw nothing but blackness, but slowly his eyes adjusted to the dim moonlight to make out Hooter's car. It was slowly rocking, and the leaf springs were creaking.

Wayne leapt up and smacked his head on the ceiling above the bed. Unless it was One-Eyed Jack in that car with Hooter, there would be hell to pay!

But first he would have to pee. Wayne cursed his aging bladder. That is why heroism is best left to the young. There are no bathroom breaks in a crisis.

Wayne stumbled down the hall toward the bathroom. It smelled like bleach. Brenda soaked her underwear in the tub. Because she could not see, the poor lady just *assumed* that her underwear were full of putrid stains. It would be embarrassing to hang them on the line to be mocked by the other wives.

Such are the anxieties of the blind.

Wayne Noodler was growing increasingly furious as he stumbled into the dark bathroom. It angered him to know that as he relieved his bladder in fits and starts, he was extending the carnal bliss in that 1970 Barracuda. When he was done urinating, he would banish Hooter from Noodler's

Bluff forever. Whoever was in that car with Hooter would be excommunicated. *How low can you go?* Wayne thought. Sleeping around like that. He demanded faithfulness from his wives. All this on his wedding day!

In the darkness, in his rage, Wayne got his feet tangled in a pair of slippery nylon panties that had fallen from the heap Brenda had tossed into the tub before bedtime. He began to lose his balance, and Wayne flailed in the darkness to catch himself on the sink, but he missed and tumbled headfirst into the bleaching underwear. His desperate reaching hand grabbed what it could—electrical cords—and he pulled the radio, curling iron, and blow-dryer in with him.

It was an old trailer. The oldest and most decrepit, because Wayne figured Brenda would never be the wiser. It was also without many safety features of a more modern trailer. Things like safety outlets with circuit breakers.

Brenda awoke when she heard the thrashing and splashing and the guttural sounds coming from the bathroom. It sounded a whole lot worse than Wayne's usual constipation. She rushed to him, deftly avoiding all obstacles, until she reached the cramped bathroom all in disarray. It smelled like burnt plastic.

She reached out toward the convulsing body, not knowing. Not seeing. And when she touched Wayne's vibrating, outstretched arm, the electricity coursed through her, too. She stiffened. She would have died, but her feet went out from under her as she slipped on the rogue panties. She fell backward and unconscious into the hall, saved by the very same pair of panties that killed Wayne Noodler.

chapter Eleven

One-Eyed Jack Lipensky decided to make an early start of it. The sun was still hidden in the east when he crept out of Twyla's trailer. He needn't have used stealth. In her near-deafness, you could start up a chain saw beside Twyla's elephantine ears and she would hear it as a gentle drone. Insomnia was never an issue with her.

Jack snooped around a bit, hoping someone would awaken. It had gotten so he took a bit of joy in performing for all the people who came to see him dowse. Even when he didn't find what he was looking for, he was sure to find *something*, so his audiences were always entertained. In his own small way, Jack made the world a better place. An audience wasn't a requirement, though. He needed an assistant, someone to dig. Jack peered into the Barracuda at the naked, sleeping Hooter. He saw the empty wine bottles. Apparently Wayne Noodler had seen fit to give two bottles of wine to a complete stranger. Jack felt betrayed. He flung open the door.

"Git up," he said.

"Huh?" Hooter realized he was naked and scrambled to cover himself.

Jack grinned. "Git up," he repeated. "I need a hand."

Literally, he did.

Hooter groaned.

"C'mon. I'll pay you half of what they pay me."

Hooter was too drunk to argue.

They found a hubcap, most of a Briggs and Stratton engine, and a hairbrush.

By then, Ernestine, Wayne's first and only *legal* wife, was sloshing water from the tank. She did not know yet that she was a widow.

"Haven't you found me a well yet, Jack?" she chided with a smile. She was pretty cheerful for having a clubfoot.

Jack grinned back. He had known Ernestine since high school. Even jitterbugged with her at the junior prom, and she wasn't bad, with her clubfoot and all. But he'd never had the courage to mix it up with girls—not until after the army, and by that time Ernestine was already taken. Eventually Jack found a good woman. But she was one of the Catholics claimed in the horrendous accident, and now he was lonely. Desperately lonely. The kind of lonely that feels like you are being slowly devoured from inside.

About that time, the bulk truck pulled up, noisily. A cloud of dust followed it and settled down as the deliveryman stepped out of the cab. Ernestine eyed Brenda's trailer, waiting for Wayne to emerge as he usually did for fuel deliveries. When he did not appear, she directed the driver to fill both tanks, even though it would have to be put on credit, and Wayne hated having any transactions on paper. He was anti-government. Like Tyrone X, he hated The Man.

Ernestine knew how Wayne hated being interrupted when he was enjoying conjugal bliss with his wives, and decided that signing the credit slip was the best of two bad choices. Amidst all the activity, Ernestine didn't notice Jack's dowsing rod jerk crazily downward and Hooter slamming at the earth wildly with a pickax.

Clank! Hooter hit rock, but Jack excitedly urged him on. Clank! Clank!

Ernestine turned just in time to see Hooter's pick come whistling down with fury. Suddenly, the pick was blasted out of his hands by the force of the liquid bursting forth, free of the earth. It showered down upon them. Jack and Hooter backed away in awe. The stuff was black. Black gold. Texas tea. The ground around the fountain pooled up into shiny black puddles.

Jack began shouting. Hooter began shouting. The bulk truck driver began shouting. And Ernestine began to jitterbug in the sand as sleepy-headed wives and children poured out of the trailers.

The racket awakened Brenda from her unconsciousness after the electrocution, and at first she could not remember what had happened. Things were very strange. She felt dizzy and had hallucinations of a dim light. But then she began to see vague shapes in the light, and she reached out to them. She touched the sink. She reached out to another fuzzy image and felt the towel bar, and realized she could see. For the first time ever, she could see!

Then she looked down into the tub and screamed. She did not scream because Wayne was dead. Mostly, she screamed at the thought that she had been sleeping with a man so hideous. It didn't help that Wayne had bleached all night. He looked quite Goth. And his hair had gone greenish blonde.

Brenda rushed screaming from her trailer. It was odd and unsettling to see things she had only felt before.

Outside, the morning sun hurt her eyes as she ran toward the voices and shapes dancing in puddles of muck. They were black and horrifying. She had no idea that's what people looked like unbleached. She screamed some more. Ernestine rushed up to her, but Brenda did not know who she was until she spoke.

"My God, dear … "

"I can see," Brenda said. "I can see!"

"It's a miracle!" Ernestine shrieked. She studied the shocked, confused woman squinting in the reddish glow of the sunrise. Brenda gazed at the scene before her. "Is that … that … water?"

"It's oil. Oil!"

"It's a miracle," Brenda said as a torrent of emotions engulfed her. Then she began sobbing. It was all so confusing. In an instant, God had answered a lifetime of prayers. She could see. And now, prosperity had come to Noodler's Bluff! For a moment she almost forgot the scene in her bathroom. She grabbed Ernestine by the shoulders and looked into her eyes for the very first time.

"Wayne is dead," she said.

And that put a damper on things.

That afternoon, morticians from Upchuck hauled Wayne away as an oil outfit from Salt Lake City tried to cap the well to keep Noodler's Bluff from being washed away by a black river. It was oil, all right. Sweet crude, and a damned miracle, but Wayne Noodler wasn't around to see it. It was hard to know how to feel about it.

By sunset Hooter was gassed up. The Goths walked over to him. They were still a little oily. With the shortage, there wasn't enough water for everyone to take a decent bath.

"Hop in if you're going," he said.

"Are you kidding?" Marcie asked. "We're rich!"

"And we don't have to marry Wayne."

Hooter couldn't decide if he was disappointed or relieved.

At this point, some readers are wondering, what does any of this have to do with Hooter's quest for his one true love, Trixie Foxalot? The answer is, nothing. But it does have something to do with Hooter. He, too, was rich, but at the moment no one knew it. So I might as well tell you what happened to everyone at Noodler's Bluff and how fortune can be smiling down on a guy like Hooter without him even seeing it.

You see, with Wayne dead and destined for a closed-casket funeral, Ernestine was the legal heir and owner of the oil. But she split everything even Steven. Lord knows, there was enough to go around.

Ernestine could finally afford a newfangled procedure and the orthopedic shoes to help her limp less. Twyla got hearing aids and grew her hair longer to cover her ears. Sandra had her goiter removed and her nose shortened. Brenda could already see. And as for Gretchen, she remained the hunchback mother of two wealthy Goths. No one yet has found a cure for hunchbacks, but one quack tried to convince Gretchen that he could build her a matching hump on her other shoulder.

"No," she said, "I'll play the hand that was dealt me."

Those are the breaks.

They were all rich. It's not like they didn't have problems, though. People think that wads of cash will solve everything, and it's just not that way. Sometimes money complicates things.

It's no big secret that One-Eyed Jack married Ernestine, who paid him for discovering oil with half of her holdings. Jack, ever true to his word, eventually paid half of what he had, which included stock in the new oil company, to Hooter. Of course, he didn't catch up to Hooter for a while, so that is how Hooter managed to drive off toward Nevada without knowing he was a millionaire. He *felt* dead broke.

Jack quit drinking after he married Ernestine. He just didn't have that many sorrows to drown anymore. And Marcie and Matilda became so cheerful, they stopped being Goth. No one was buying it anyway. Lots of other stuff happened to the rest of them, but that's all you need to know.

You know, I feel pretty good about the way things worked out.

chapter *Twelve*

Dear Hooter,

It is as if Trixie Foxalot is speaking to me from the television. She was screaming because her boyfriend got killed. She looked great.

Sincerely,
Hooter

Thus the entry into Hooter Pridley's journal on his first morning in Charming, Nevada. He was in a twenty-dollar flophouse outside of Carson City.

You're probably wondering about Trixie Foxalot's dead boyfriend and the screaming. Here's the deal. Hooter fell asleep while watching television. Halfway through the *Dawn of the Cannibal Night Freaks*, Hooter woke up to the angelic visage of Trixie Foxalot in a virginal-white low-cut sweater. She crept up the attic steps looking for her boyfriend, thereby violating a cardinal rule of all scary movies—never, *never* go into the attic or the basement alone. Heck, some women won't even go to the bathroom alone.

But not Trixie Foxalot. She found her boyfriend, all right—the killer had run a half-inch drill through his brain. When he was not engaged in cannibalism, the killer was a skilled carpenter. As one might imagine, Trixie was horrified to see her boyfriend lurching around in his letterman's sweater, drooling and grinning moronically as his brains leaked out of the circular hole in his forehead. Now that is a date gone awry. You couldn't blame Trixie for screaming.

Her breasts heaved and seemed to swell as she screamed into the camera. She had nice teeth. It was a wonderful, shrill scream. It sounded like the opera singers you see on public television, except no one is coming after them with a bloody drill. They just scream because they're on public television. Trixie's scream continued a full half second after her mouth closed, but Hooter did not notice.

He slept fitfully after that, and he dreamed. He dreamed about bathrooms—bathrooms in high school gyms, bathrooms in gas stations, and bathrooms in stores, and every one of them was occupied, and, boy, did Hooter have to go.

Then he woke up and went to the bathroom.

Later, as he was brushing his teeth, Hooter realized he had successfully analyzed his first dream. Sigmund Freud, pshaw! There was nothing to it.

• • •

The other rooms were still dark when Hooter walked, freshly showered, along the outside doors of the Raging Steer Motel at five-thirty in the morning. Hooter figured the steer was raging because he was a steer. The procedure is supposed to make you docile, and maybe it does. But in the beginning, it would sure tick you off. Hooter heard a rhythmic banging from room 113 and accompanying grunts. It sounded like someone was getting beat up in there.

Snake Western didn't look up from his cards when Hooter dropped the keys on the counter. Snake was the night clerk at the Raging Steer, and he had two pair—jacks and deuces. You couldn't see his eyes beneath a grungy gray felt cowboy hat pitched low, its wings rolled slightly and tucked tight against the crown.

"I'm in," he said, tossing a dollar into the pot.

Hooter watched with interest.

A massive, bearded trucker, a good foot wider on both sides than his chair, raised Snake fifty cents. A man named Apache, wearing a Red Sox cap, was seemingly asleep, his legs splayed out beneath the table. He tilted his head back so he could see out of his slits, and he raised the trucker. And so it went until the trucker's wallet was empty.

"Take two lugs of oranges?" he asked Snake. "California navels. Good uns."

Snake nodded. It was a bet. He was almost out of oranges from the last time. His girlfriend liked them. The good thing about oranges is that they prevent scurvy. Which is why you don't see much scurvy nowadays.

"I'll call, then," the trucker said. He had three aces.

Snake's deuces and jacks weren't enough. But Apache had a full house.

"Gosh darn," the trucker said, rising. "Double dagnabbit!"

"Same time next week, Peterbilt?" Snake asked. He was bad with names. He named everyone after the vehicle they drove.

"Yup," Peterbilt said as he headed out.

Hooter stepped aside so the man could angle out the door.

Hooter began to follow him when Snake called out, "Hey, 'Cuda."

Hooter pointed to his chest.

"Yeah, you. Come here, 'Cuda. Ever play any cards?"

"A little Go Fish when I was a kid."

"That'll do, won't it, Apache?"

Apache nodded. His hair was so greasy, his cap barely moved as the head nodded beneath it. Languidly, he slid the pile of coins and crumpled bills from the center of the table and began pocketing the money.

Hooter won the next five hands and ninety-eight dollars. He let Snake keep the oranges.

"Beginner's luck, huh, Apache?" Snake asked.

Apache grunted as they watched Hooter count the money into his wallet.

Hooter liked an organized billfold. Ones to the front, hundreds to the back ... There were five crisp hundreds and a handful of twenties. A little less than a thousand dollars in all. No credit cards. Hooter's grandpa didn't believe in them, so Hooter didn't either.

Suddenly a crashing noise came from the doorway. A man walked smack into the glass door, fell down, and from his knees swatted at the handle. When he finally grasped it, he tried to use it to pull himself back up, but the door opened toward him and he went rolling back into the gutter.

Hooter tucked his money away. He stared.

On his next try, the man made it through the door, stumbling as if walking on borrowed legs, before slamming into the counter. Clinging to the counter like a drowning man, he swayed unsteadily around it, fell to his knees again, and began heaving violently into the waste can. The sound of impaled dinosaurs came from behind the counter, followed by deep gasps, coughing, and spitting.

"That's Yugo," Snake explained. "He's got day shift."

"Think he'll make it?" Hooter asked.

"Shore," Snake said. "This is one of his better days."

The stench of puke wafted toward the table. A whistling, wheezing sound echoed from the wastebasket.

Hooter turned pale and stood on wobbly legs as his own stomach churned. "I gotta go."

Once, at a party when Gladys Neidermeyer threw up purple wine on a white carpet, he tried gallantly to mop it up, but ended up throwing up too. Which set her off again. So they left the party barfing together. They were not invited back. Now Hooter felt the taste of bile in the back of his throat. He rushed out the door.

It was not until he sucked in a lungful of air that he realized just how long he had been holding his breath. Even his Barracuda sputtered asthmatically as Hooter warmed the engine in the desert chill.

Hooter fiddled hopelessly for some radio station that was not playing country music before settling on Paul Harvey, who was selling a mattress that would change your life and possibly revolutionize the art of sleeping.

When he looked up from the radio, he saw Snake limping along the only road out of town. (Hooter, I mean. He's the one who spotted old Snake. Not Paul Harvey. Paul is just a one-time plot element to add ambiance and a sense of place to the book. Besides, I got a mattress out of the deal.)

It was more than a limp. It was agony just to watch Snake walk. His right leg was stiff as a board, and he swung it in a circular motion. The boot dragged in the dirt, and then the process was repeated.

Snake had hobbled a good hundred yards when Hooter eased to a stop beside him.

"Need a lift?" The Barracuda rumbled softly but threateningly beneath his voice.

"Nah. I'm fine." Snake gazed out into the horizon, majestic in his misery. "Just fine."

"Where you going?" Hooter asked.

"Day job. At the ranch."

"Where is it?"

"Not far. Maybe three miles."

"Get in."

"Much obliged."

In spite of himself, Hooter found himself staring at Snake Western's leg as he eased the thing, like a log, into the car. Hooter tried to imagine what orthopedic horrors were hidden by the faded, impossibly narrow jeans.

"Rodeo," Snake said.

"Huh?"

Snake nodded at the leg. "Rodeo."

"Hmm."

"I was pretty good, too. Made some nice paychecks. *Niiice* purses. But them days is gone."

They drove slowly to the east. Hooter squinted into the rising sun.

"Almost lost it," Snake said.

"What?"

Snake nodded to the leg.

"Yeah?" Hooter asked.

"I don't like to talk about it, though."

"Okay."

"The doc said it was the worst wreck he had ever seen. The absolute worst. I don't even like to think about it."

Hooter nodded.

"Lotsa guys git busted up," Snake said. "You just gotta cowboy up. No sense in making a big deal about it."

In the distance Hooter could make out a dilapidated two-story building with a greenish glow emanating from the side facing the road.

"I paid him, though," Snake said.

"Who?"

"The doc. Every cent. After all, he saved my leg. Had to sell my car, even."

But by now Hooter was fascinated with what he saw. The ranch was called Ruby's Bunkhouse. That's what the huge neon sign said. A flashing pink neon cowgirl grinned out at the new morning. She had six-shooters in her hands. When she leaned over, her skirt flew up and exposed her rear. When she stood, she blew puffs of smoke away from the barrels of the guns. Hooter recognized phallic implications from his crash course on Freud.

As he pulled closer, Hooter could read the smaller sign in the yard: Twofer Tuesdays or half price on one.

"Two what?" Hooter asked.

"Girls," Snake said with a leer.

It was Tuesday.

chapter Thirteen

There was a mannequin behind the counter staring motion-less at the door when Hooter followed Snake Western into Ruby's Bunkhouse. Hooter wondered why anyone would make a mannequin so haggard looking, with a face of plaster, badly dyed black hair, and a fake eyelash that had come unglued and no longer followed the curve of the eye.

Then the mannequin spoke and startled Hooter. "Mornin', Snake," the mannequin said. "Want me to call Glenda up front?"

"Nope. I'm busted."

"Suit yourself. You know your shift don't start for an hour. I ain't gonna start payin' you until then."

Snake nodded. "Glenda's my girl," he explained to Hooter. "Least she used to be. Until I busted up my leg and got destitute. I'm trying to win her back, but the only way I can see her is to pay. I have to wait until Tuesdays so I can afford it. Of course, the card game settled that … "

In a way, Hooter thought it was romantic. Romantic like falling in love with a calendar. "How much you need?" he asked.

"Two hundred."

"That's *half* price?"

"Yeah, but you should see her."

Hooter opened his wallet. Snake waved him off, but he

seemed moved by the offer. "I couldn't," he said. "Wouldn't be right. Be too much like charity."

"Call it a loan," Hooter said.

The mannequin called for Glenda, and boy, she was something—a raven-haired beauty with ample curves and milky white flesh in black lace. She slouched in unenthusiastically.

"Snake," she said flatly. That was the greeting.

"Glenda." Snake touched the brim of his hat.

"This is business," Glenda said. "That's all. Nothing more."

Snake nodded. He turned to Hooter. "What about you? It's Twofer Tuesday."

One thing about Hooter, he liked a bargain, and if the girls resembled Glenda, then perhaps LA could wait a few hours more.

The lineup filtered out from doors and hallways, and not one of them looked like Glenda. In fact, they favored the mannequin. Hooter instantly regretted his decision, but he had no intention of walking out. That would be an insult. Hooter's mother had taught him manners, though she had never envisioned these particular circumstances.

He smiled gamely at the fortyish hags. There were seven of them. One thing was certain: he wasn't picking *two* of them. To hell with Twofer Tuesday. He glanced back at the counter, because the mannequin was starting to look better all the time. He was about to ask for her when he spotted movement deep in the dark hallway. His pulse quickened.

She was young and slender and blonde and wearing a Catholic schoolgirl getup. Hooter wished she would step into the light.

Then the front door of the brothel opened. It was Apache, and Hooter's desperation grew. What if Apache wanted the only decent whore in the place?

"I'll take her," Hooter said, pointing into the hallway.

"You don't want *her*," Snake whispered.

Apache peered down the hall with interest.

"I want *her*," Hooter said firmly.

"Cy, you got a date," the mannequin said, and the girl stepped into the light. She wore black, flat, one-buckle schoolgirl shoes, white stockings to her mid-thighs, a short plaid skirt, and a red vest over a long-sleeved blouse. Hooter's eyes worked up past her fantastic legs. Her blouse was open three buttons down, and the rounds of her breasts were visible. She had a ponytail.

And a wart—a monstrous wart in the center of her forehead.

Snake shot Hooter an "I told you so" glance and limped along behind the fabulous, disinterested Glenda. Hooter glumly followed Cyclops into the dark hallway. Apache grinned.

The sheets were in a heap. Barry White crooned mockingly through crackly speakers.

> *The first, the last, my everything,*
> *And the answer to all my dreams.*

Hooter's eyes were fixated on the wart. It was the size of two pencil erasers and about that color. It was pink, smooth, and shiny, as if she polished it.

"Two hundred for the basic," she said. "No funny stuff."

"Huh? Oh, yeah." He fished into his wallet, thumbed to the back, and pulled out two bills without his eyes ever leaving her wart.

She put the bills on the dresser, then asked him to undress and inspected him.

It wasn't easy. His genitalia had sucked up into his stomach. When she was satisfied he wasn't diseased, she wiped him with a washcloth and disrobed herself.

She eased onto the bed beside him. She smelled vaguely of Pine-Sol.

Hooter closed his eyes and tried to concentrate on the gentle tugging fingers, but the vision of the wart would not desist. His penis remained in full retreat, despite heroic measures to lure it into the fray.

In time, the hands moved away and the bed began shaking slightly, keeping time to a soft whimpering. Hooter opened his eyes. The girl's eyes were red. She sniffled.

"It's me, isn't it?" She sobbed some more.

"What do you mean?" Hooter asked, playing dumb, which wasn't a real stretch.

"My wart. That's it, isn't it?"

"I didn't even notice," Hooter said, now sitting up.

"Don't lie to me! You think I don't know I'm a freak?"

Hooter shuddered inwardly and looped his arm around the Cyclops. "I'll still pay you," he said.

"I wasn't always a … a … a … "

"A whore?" Hooter added helpfully.

Now she had began wailing loudly. Hooter feared everyone would hear. He pulled her closer so his chest would muffle the sound.

When she had composed herself, she stroked his face. "You're nice," she said. "Not like the others. You don't have to pay me. I'll pay the house myself."

"The house?"

"The house gets half. But don't worry about that. The operation can wait a few more weeks."

"Operation?"

"The wart. I'm saving up to have it removed. Then I can get out of this business and go back to school. I want to be a veterinarian. And help animals. But that's not your concern. You can go. I know you can't stand the sight of me."

"How much more do you need for the operation?"

"Five hundred. But … but … " She began crying again.

"But what?"

"But hardly anyone ever picks me. Only the really drunk ones."

Hooter slid back into his pants and put on his shirt. He slid out his wallet and gallantly counted out five hundred dollars and laid it beside the other two hundred.

At this, the girl threw her arms around him. "I don't know what to say," she said.

• • •

Hooter Pridley was feeling mighty noble when he drove away from Ruby's Bunkhouse that morning, even though he was nine hundred dollars poorer. His mother might have said he committed the sin of pride. But didn't *she* feel a sense of pride in her sacrifices to the big-haired preacher on television? It's human nature to feel good about doing good deeds. That's what keeps us doing them. Some of us give to televangelists. Others give to whores and cowboys with bum legs.

Hooter smiled to himself when he considered one other thing: he had not cheated on Trixie Foxalot. For the first time in his life, he had held a naked woman in his arms and had not been compelled to have sex with her. It was evident he truly was in love with Trixie Foxalot. Sure, maybe the wart had something to do with it, but everyone deserves the benefit of the doubt every now and then.

And what of the wart? Was the surgery a success? Hooter Pridley never learned the answer, though sometimes in his old age he wondered how things worked out for the girl. The memory always made him feel good. But just because Hooter never knew what happened after he drove off is no reason not to tell you.

When they heard the rumble of the Barracuda fade, Snake and Glenda emerged from her room, looking decidedly unmussed, to join the mannequin and Apache at the table. They were drinking rewarmed bitter coffee.

Glenda kissed Apache. "Hi, baby." She looked outside and saw his gleaming yellow 1959 Chevy pickup. "Got it running again, huh? Does that mean we get to go to the drive-in tonight?"

"Yup," Apache said.

Cyclops drifted in from the hallway, plopped into Snake's lap, and kissed him deeply.

"Want some coffee?" he asked.

She did, and the mannequin poured.

"How much did you get?" Snake asked.

"A hundred. Plus two hundred more for the wart."

They divvied up the money, including Snake's two-hundred-dollar loan.

"Did you get the oranges?" Cyclops asked, staring absently at her reflection in the smudged black Formica table.

"Two lugs."

"I love you, baby," she said. "And I love oranges. But next time, I'm not doing Peterbilt. I think he cracked my ribs." She stared some more at her reflection. Even she was hypnotized by the wart. "I've been thinking ... maybe I really ought to get this thing removed."

"*No!*" the other four said in unison.

"It's what's on the inside that counts," the mannequin said in her most motherly fashion.

"I love you just the way you are," Snake added.

"Can't hardly see it," Glenda said.

Outside, a car pulled up. Four car doors slammed.

"More conventioneers," Cyclops said. "I'd better go freshen up."

"And I'm going home," the mannequin said.

Cyclops vanished into the darkness, followed by Glenda.

"You got it from here?" the mannequin asked Snake as four bleary-eyed men in rumpled business suits walked in.

"Shore," he said.

"Think Cy's holding out on us?"

"I expect," Snake said. "A rube like that … she coulda got twice as much. But I'll steal it back from her tonight." He rose and walked—without a limp—to his station behind the counter.

And so it goes.

Maybe you're disappointed with the way things worked out in Charming, Nevada. I was when I found out. You always hope people will do the right thing. But there are a few certainties in life: death, taxes, and the fact that you can never trust a guy named Snake.

If you want to look into the future a few decades, I can tell you that Cyclops never did have the wart removed. She never became a veterinarian either. Time passed. They kept running the scam until she was no longer young, and even a schoolgirl's outfit and a dark hallway couldn't fool the drunkest johns. By then, she couldn't have afforded the operation anyway. What would it have improved? She decayed like mulch until the wart was her best feature. She died bitter and lonely. From scurvy.

A few years later Snake was run over by a truck hauling citrus fruit, and he lost a leg. Say what you will about God, but he has a good sense of irony. Infection set in, but Snake Western fought a good long while before it did him in.

Apache and Glenda got out of the racket and took up selling Amway.

I never heard what happened to the mannequin. She must be dead by now.

Some stories end happier than others. Sometimes I just want to reach into this book and slap these people around and set them straight. But all I can do is tell the story like it happened. Even if I did appear on a black Formica tabletop in some Nevada whorehouse like a prophet of doom, kicking over the coffee and shaking my finger, do you think they would listen?

No. They might straighten up for a while. But they would backslide into doing what comes natural to them. A dog is a dog. A snake will always be a snake. You can no more change people than you can change the location of the stars. You can remove all the warts you want, but what is inside will remain the same.

People will disappoint you, but it's not my fault.

Maybe you think it's my job to take care of Hooter Pridley too. Maybe you feel *just terrible* that poor old misguided Hooter Pridley headed off to Los Angeles with less than a hundred dollars in his pocket.

But you already know that Hooter will find his true love. You know that a one-armed Methodist in Utah will eventually make him a millionaire. And anyway, we shouldn't lose sight of the fact that Hooter felt *really good* about the deeds he had done. Sure, things were not what they seemed to be, but does that matter? Things are hardly *ever* what they seem to be. We might be an alien experiment—the equivalent of an ant farm in a nerd's room. Maybe L. Ron Hubbard has it right. The way I see it, reality is a deeply personal thing.

Just because Hooter Pridley was unknowingly tricked doesn't make what he did any less noble. When it comes right down to it, in spite of his many flaws, Hooter Pridley had a good heart.

And I think God watches out for people like that.

chapter Fourteen

You can't believe the cars. That's the thing about LA. It seemed to Hooter as if every car was a BMW, a Rolls Royce, or a Mercedes, all gleaming in the California sun. A car in California is as much a status symbol as a trophy wife and a membership at the right country club. Hooter felt a bit insignificant as he stared at the marvelous machines in the lanes around him. The volume of traffic was overwhelming at first, but Hooter quickly realized that his magnificent Barracuda had a distinct advantage: power. Soon he was gliding in and out of lanes and threading through the pack.

In time he noticed people staring at him. *At his car.* He felt self-conscious, as if the Barracuda wasn't worthy. But he realized soon enough that these were not disdainful stares, but those of admiration. A man in a candy apple red 1963 Chevy lowrider with zebra-skin seats, a fur-covered dash, and a steering wheel made of chrome chains pulled up beside him and saluted the car. Hooter was in. The newest member of the California Car Club.

He had no idea where he was going. But he had a full tank of gas, thirty-five dollars, and a coupon for a free Coke with a car wash. He was just driving, baby.

He thought that maybe the smile from the platinum blonde in the powder blue BMW was aimed at him. They *were* a handsome couple, Hooter and the car. Hooter, with a vacant stare that made him seem mysterious and deep, and that wonderful 1970 Barracuda that exuded power.

He had restored it lovingly over the course of six long years. It was not stock. He had put in a racing clutch he got free from the parts salesman as a kickback for buying his brand. The engine was a marvel of gleaming chrome, tuned to fly off the line. The rear-end ratio made it unbeatable in the quarter mile in Sterling, Colorado. The rear fenders had been reworked to allow two inches of slicks to protrude. The seats were white leather, the carpeting black, the windows tinted.

Like all American men, Hooter loved his car, and on the days when he and Gladys Neidermeyer argued, if you would have asked him to choose between her and the car, it would have been close. There is a sacred primal connection between man and machine. Seriously. The first chance man had to invent something, he made the wheel.

Hooter drove with no destination in mind, just a fuzzy plan to win over Trixie Foxalot, when suddenly he saw a sign. Literally. Up ahead, on metal stilts fifty feet high, in blinding yellow, there was a sign. Hooter spotted it, and it was almost biblical in significance. Crazy Sheldon was selling discount electronics two exits up. *He* would know how to find Trixie Foxalot.

The Lord works in mysterious ways—often through people with very big hair—but he uses signs, too. Most of them are more subtle than neon yellow fifty-footers.

I guess God figured Hooter needed something obvious.

God doesn't do burning bushes anymore. You have to change with the times. No one listens to burning bushes these days, anyway. They're too busy yapping on cell phones. And even if they noticed one, they would just call the fire department.

• • •

Crazy Sheldon's was a madhouse. Sweating salesmen with untucked shirts chased consumers down the aisles. They were working on commission. Hooter tried to flag one of them down, but he was on the hunt—a woman in shades and a fake fur. She looked loaded. But another salesman got there first.

Resigned to dealing with a pauper, he turned to Hooter. "Whatta ya need, bub?"

"I'm looking for someone."

"Look, you want answers, you gotta buy something."

Hooter picked up a boom box. It had flashing red lights to show how powerful it was, and it was marked down from one hundred twenty-nine dollars to just twenty-five dollars. Including tax.

"I'll take this," Hooter said.

The salesman sniffed contemptuously and made his way to the long line of cash registers.

"I'd like to speak to Crazy Sheldon, please," Hooter said.

The man rang up the sale at the cash register. "Ain't here," he said without looking up.

"Where is he, then?"

"Look, there *is* no Crazy Sheldon."

"But I saw him on television."

The salesman threw up his hands and began walking back to the big-screen televisions.

Hooter hustled behind. "But I *saw* him on television!"

"Look, doofus, it's an actor. It's shtick. Get it?"

"Who owns the store, then?"

The guy shrugged. "The Heebs, I guess."

Hooter had no idea who the Heebs were. It kind of rang a bell, but he wasn't going to ask and end up looking like a complete idiot. Besides, he sensed the man had the patience for only one more question. If that.

"Do you know where can I find Trixie Foxalot?" Hooter ventured.

"Never heard of her," the man said. And off he went.

How could you live in Los Angeles and not know who Trixie Foxalot was? She was a star, for crissakes! She was the most beautiful blond in a sea of blondes, a princess of peace!

With ten dollars in his pocket and a really keen boom box, Hooter slunk back to his car. The paint looked less shiny, somehow, and the world felt darker.

It was nearly dark when Hooter parked just off Sunset Boulevard among the dealers, hookers, and hustlers. There was a bald man with a neat white goatee playing clarinet at the corner. A box of coins and wrinkled greenbacks lay at his feet. A sign reading War Is Over was taped to the box. Hooter stood and listened, an audience of one. The song was a lament, but a beautiful one. The clarinet player looked at the box, and his gentle message was clear: admission required.

Hooter was touched by the song and by the sign that so beautifully echoed Trixie Foxalot's fondest wish, for world peace. Hooter pulled open his almost-empty wallet. The distinguished old man watched him pull out the last ten-dollar bill. It floated down into the box. Hooter listened for a few moments more, closing his eyes and drifting with the melody. Then he continued his walk to nowhere in the fading light.

He was snapped out of his reverie by a ruckus and the old man's shout behind him.

A tall man with a pockmarked face in a long coat yelled at the old man, "How many times I tell you? This is my corner!" He kicked the old man's box, and the coins and dollars flew. The pockmarked man continued walking as the old man scrambled for the money.

The breeze lifted Hooter's ten-dollar bill and floated it to him, almost taunting him to reach for it. He did, and missed, and then it took off as if rocket-propelled, leading him nearly a block.

The old man watched the chase dispiritedly. Whether

Hooter caught it or not was a moot point. The old man figured the money was gone.

Finally, with a well-placed stomp, Hooter stopped the skittering ten-dollar bill. Without hesitation he walked back to the incredulous clarinet player and handed him the money. "You got the rest?"

"Yes," the man said.

"That guy's an asshole," Hooter said. He didn't usually speak badly about anyone, but he had had a hard day and a fact is a fact.

"Ivan? Yes, a fair description. He runs a three-card monte game up the street. He's Russian. Or Lithuanian. Anyway, I used to work the spot where he's at now. There is shade most of the day. He chased me down here. Now he just wants me gone. I don't know why. I don't cut into his business much. I've seen him take tourists five hundred bucks a shot. ... Don't *you* play him! It's a sucker bet."

"Can't anyway," Hooter said.

The old man remembered Hooter's bare wallet. "You gave me your last ten bucks?"

Hooter nodded.

"You workin' me, boy? 'Cause, if you are, I'll know. There's not a scam down here I haven't seen a million times or didn't invent myself before I went straight."

"No, sir."

The old man looked long and hard into Hooter's tired eyes. Hard to fake that.

"Here, take this," he said, shoving forty-five dollars into Hooter's hands. "For two hundred, you can get a week's room and board at Maggie's. It's four blocks that way. It's a real shithole, but there's running water and enough food to starve on."

Great, Hooter thought, *I'm a hundred and fifty-five dollars short of a week in a shithole.*

"I'll tell you how you can get the rest," the old man said with a sly smile. "Play Ivan."

"You said not to."

"Who you gonna listen to? Me or me?"

For the first time in hours, Hooter found a reason to smile.

"Listen careful, now," the clarinet player said. "You only got one chance. If you do it right, he won't play you again. Use the five ones first. He'll piss and moan about you being so cheap, but don't bet more than a buck. Make sure he sees the other forty bucks, though. You follow his hand real close. On those first five bets, you pick the one you think is the queen of hearts. You'll be wrong, of course."

"What if I'm right?"

"You won't be. Ivan's the best three-card monte player I ever saw. *Ever.* But he has a weakness. Everyone has a weakness. Listen up, now. After you lose the first five dollars, you start to walk away. This will drive Ivan up a wall. He'll call you back. He'll give you better odds. See, Ivan don't like it unless he can take each sucker for at least ten bucks. It's his game within the game, see? Don't go back until he gives you ten to one—and he will. *Then* you lay down the forty. When there's big money on the line, he always goes to a special shuffle. The Magic Betty. Magic Betty ain't ever been beat."

The plan had sounded good up to this point. Now Hooter decided the man was completely nuts. He started to walk away.

"Hang with me," the old man said, tugging on Hooter's jacket. "When Ivan's done, you pick the card on the left. It's *always* the one on the left. The left! Hear me now! It looks slow and easy, and you are going to think it's the middle card. Do not believe your eyes. Believe me."

"What if I win and he doesn't give me the money?"

"He'll give you the money. He's a cheating sack of shit, but he ain't a welsher."

Ivan spotted Hooter and his vacant stare half a block away.

"Yo, yo! You! You wanna play a little game?" He began an easy shuffle. "We'll practice. Here's the queen. You follow her around. Yes, yes, that's it. Now which one is it?"

Hooter pointed.

He was right.

Maybe the old man *didn't* know everything.

"Ohh. *Impressive*. A prodigy! What you say, sport? We do the next one for a ten spot?"

Hooter counted his meager holdings so Ivan could see. He shook his head.

"What? You got no guts, man. You gotta live on the wild side."

Hooter laid a dollar onto the small table.

Ivan sneered. He was going to have to work for it. In five hands he had five dollars, each win accompanied by more insults to Hooter's manhood.

"Another *whole* dollar," Ivan said as he pocketed the last of the five. "When you gonna run with the big dogs?"

Hooter's face turned red. He had never been one to back away from any fight, any competition. He was all-conference football. All-conference baseball. All-goddamn-conference wrestling. He *hated* losing. Hated it. Still, he swallowed hard and turned away.

"Come back," Ivan called. "I'll give you five to one!"

Hooter kept walking.

"I guess we know who's boss, eh!" Ivan hooted. "Ten to one, loser!"

But now Hooter was so mad, he didn't even want to play the son of a bitch.

"Twenty to one!"

Hooter kept walking.

"Fifty to one, chickenshit."

Hooter slowed his walk.

"Gutless!" Ivan said.

Hooter whirled around. His eyes were no longer vacant.

They were ablaze. "You say something, Rooskie?" He clenched his fists.

"Easy, boy. I just wanna have a little game. That's all." The tone was soothing. "I was just messin' with you, man. … And anyway, I'm Lithuanian."

Hooter's anger eased. "Uh, sorry."

"No big thing. Happens all the time. Just a case of mistooken identity. Just like I mistook you for a big-time player."

"Fifty to one?"

"That's what I said."

Hooter laid down the two twenties, emptying his wallet for the second time in thirty minutes.

Ivan got a tick under his eye. What the hell had he been thinking? He had been so intent on getting Hooter to lose his composure, he had lost his own for an instant.

For an instant.

Pride would not allow him to limit the bet. And Betty had never been beaten. Thank God for Betty. "Okay, here we go. It's Magic Betty time!"

Suddenly Hooter had an awful thought: *Whose left? His or Ivan's?* But the cards were already moving. Every few rotations, Ivan showed Hooter the queen before slowly shuffling her along. Finally he was done. Hooter's eyes had followed the queen to the middle, but he remembered the old man's words: "It's always the one on the left."

But which left?

"You gonna pick a card or we gonna stand here all night?" Ivan said. His voice had hardened again.

Hooter's hand hovered over the card on Ivan's left. The tick in Ivan's cheek slowed. Hooter exhaled deeply and moved his hand to the card on his own left. It hovered there. He swallowed hard and pointed.

Ivan blanched as he flipped the card. Queen of fucking hearts.

The tick returned as a full-blown palsy.

Ivan pulled wads of cash from his socks and from inside his coat until he had counted out two thousand dollars into Hooter's palm. He swore with great fervor in Russian. Or Lithuanian. Maybe both. Glumly, he watched Hooter walk back toward the old man, who was leaning against the wall in a confident pose.

"You told him, didn't you, you old bastard! *You told him!*" Ivan screamed. His coat billowed in the breeze, giving him the appearance of a diseased buzzard.

The old man smiled and began to play. It was a lovely tune with a Russian lilt.

Definitely Russian.

And Hooter began to dance.

chapter **Fifteen**

Maggie's was a shithole. It made the run-down whorehouse in Charming, Nevada, look like Buckingham Palace, and by comparison, Maggie made the mannequin look like Raquel Welch. The beds were teeming with crawling things. Other things slithered out of the drain when Hooter tried to scrub off the vermin he had picked up in bed. No television. No radio. The window didn't open, but the glass was broken, so it didn't matter.

Breakfast was a scoop of undercooked eggs with bits of Spam mixed in. For fifty cents extra, you could have a day-old donut. Maggie had stringy gray hair and a body so wrinkled and flabby beneath an oversized wrinkled, stained housedress, one could not tell where the dress began and the body ended. She had evidently been truant from charm school.

"Hey, you drag-ass pieces of shit! You good-for-nothing bums!"

And good morning to you, ma'am.

"When you get done, you bus the tables! Scrape the leftovers into that can there. Put the plates here. Any questions, scumbags?"

There was a general moaning from the oppressed. There were about a dozen of them packed around two discarded school lunchroom tables.

"Zip the lips, you reprobates! I'll kick your asses out, and then what will you do?"

Sink to the ground and say, "Free at last! Thank God Almighty, I'm free at last!" Hooter thought. When he was done, he dutifully bused his table and stood before the disgusting Maggie until she noticed him.

"What can I do for you, Fresh Meat?"

"Can you tell me how to find the Heebs?"

"The Heebs!"

"Yes, ma'am," Hooter said.

"Hey, Beezer, get a load of this! The kid's looking for Heebs!"

"Shalom," Beezer said, and he and Maggie laughed.

To be fair, in Sterling, Colorado, there was a family called the Hiebs. They were famous in a local kind of way. They sang with matching costumes and unmatched voices at church suppers and such. Hooter was thinking along those lines.

Maggie shrugged and pointed through the grungy window to a gleaming gold dome on the skyline, several blocks away. "That's where you'll find more Heebs than you can shake a stick at."

Even at that distance, the grandeur of the building was evident. *These California Heebs must be loaded.* Hooter walked with his eyes fixed on the gleaming building.

Hooter turned the corner to find the Barracuda. The spot was bare. He looked on surrounding blocks, thinking that perhaps he had just misjudged the location. But no, the car was gone. A sense of dread crept up from his bowels as he walked the blocks around Maggie's Shithole. After he had paced every street in a three-block radius, he looked for a pay phone. The ones he found were mutilated shreds of plastic and frayed wires. Someone in the neighborhood had a grudge against the phone company. Imagine that.

Hooter couldn't remember when he had felt so low. Not since Gladys Neidermeyer hit him in the nose with a dildo and threw his underwear in a tree. His increasingly panicked circling led him to within a block of the majestic golden dome of the Heeb mansion. Perhaps they could help.

No one came when he knocked. The door was so thick and heavy, he doubted anyone inside could hear. But it was open, and he slowly pushed his way in. A boy of about sixteen was polishing the woodwork in a cavernous auditorium of some sort. The boy saw Hooter's bare head and urgent stare, and he sensed trouble. He began to retreat toward the rabbi's office.

"I'm looking for the Heebs!" Hooter shouted, starting after him. The shout echoed back to Hooter, louder upon its return. It sounded deep and threatening. The boy accelerated.

Hooter was nearly to the passageway into which the boy had sprinted when a door opened and a strapping man stepped out. The boy cowered behind him.

"Good morning," the man said evenly. "I'm Rabbi Goldberg. How can I help you?"

"I'm looking for the Heebs," Hooter repeated.

The rabbi's chest heaved. He had been a Golden Gloves champion. He stepped closer to Hooter, with a hint of menace. "Maybe you need to find the niggers, spics, wops, and chinks, too."

"No. Just the Heebs," the oblivious Hooter said. "Are you a Heeb?"

The rabbi studied Hooter. Was he just loopy or a threat?

"Are you a goy?" he retorted.

"No, I'm a Pridley," Hooter said. "Of the Colorado Pridleys."

The rabbi's chest began vibrating. He tilted his head back. The boy behind him knew what was coming: laughter.

Rabbi Goldberg howled, and when he saw Hooter's confusion, he roared some more. "Oy! A comedian, we have, eh, Simon?"

Hooter hadn't intended humor, but it was better than an insult, and he hadn't intended that, either. He instantly liked Goldberg. His long face was crowned by curly black hair and accented with round spectacles and big, straight teeth that dominated his face when he smiled. He was smiling now as he studied the slightly disheveled Hooter.

"Come. Come to my office. What did you say your name was?"

"Hooter."

"Ah, yes. Of course. *Hooter.*" He smiled some more, but the boy remained distrustful. "It's all right, Simon. Finish your work."

The rabbi's office walls were covered with Dodgers memorabilia, including a personalized photo of Tommy Lasorda. A bulletin board bristled with reminders. There was a fund-raiser to send a contingent of the eldest of the synagogue on their first visit to Jerusalem. Yom Kippur next week. A bake sale after that.

Hooter was at ease talking to Rabbi Goldberg. He told of his quest to find Trixie Foxalot and the loss of his car and the fact that it felt like things were crawling in his hair. He told about the nonexistent Crazy Sheldon and the clarinet player on the corner. He didn't get into specifics about the dildo, the Mormon Goths, or the Nevada Cyclops. After all, Goldberg was a man of God.

"Hooter," the rabbi said sympathetically, "I cannot tell you where to find this woman or even if you *should* find her. In matters of the heart, you must listen to the heart and not myopic rabbis. What looks senseless to one is an epiphany to another. It might do you some good to examine *why* you are so set on this woman who screams at you from the television and does commercials with men who do not exist."

"I want to make her happy," Hooter said.

"I see. Is that so? You wish to make a total stranger happy? You think you could make *me* happy?"

"No. I don't know what would make you happy."

"Well, my friend, I will tell you what I know. No person can make another person happy." He paused for effect. "But one person can surely make another miserable."

"That doesn't seem quite fair," Hooter said.

"Fair, schmair! It is what it is. But enough. You figure it out. I have enough problems. I have thirteen elders lined up for Jerusalem and only the funding for eleven. And between you and me, a couple of them have the money to pay their own way. But that's my worry. I think maybe I can help you with your car, though. … Simon! Come here!"

The boy appeared almost instantly. He had been eavesdropping.

"You want me to speak up next time or do you want to sit in on the next meeting?" Goldberg asked.

The boy hung his head.

"Mr. Pridley here, of the Colorado Pridleys, has lost his car. He was parked near Maggie's."

The boy nodded knowingly.

"You see if you can find the man his car." Goldberg turned to Hooter. "You got money?"

"How much do I need?"

"Two hundred fifty."

"I got that."

"Go, then."

The car had been impounded inside a fenced lot at Bernie's Towing. It sat gleaming and unharmed inside the ten-foot wire-mesh fence. Hooter was in a joyful mood.

"They clean the streets every Wednesday morning," Simon explained. "No parking."

"I didn't see a sign," Hooter said.

"Bernie pays the bums to tear them down."

Even that didn't temper Hooter's joy. Two hundred fifty dollars for the return of the Barracuda? It was a bargain.

Bernie chewed a cigar stub as he scrawled out a receipt. "Number 33. If anything's missing, we ain't responsible."

Hooter drove the car to the synagogue. Rabbi Goldberg was changing the letters on the sign out front. Simon got out. The rabbi walked to the car, his lips pursed in a whistle. Hooter turned the key off so they could talk.

Goldberg stroked the orange fender. "How many coats of paint?"

"Six."

"I see now why you were so worried. This is more than a car. It's a jewel. Four twenty-six? Bored out, I bet."

"You know cars," Hooter said.

"I had a 1968 Road Runner once. Purple. Hood scoop. Spoiler. A real flyer."

"What happened to it?"

"Sold it. I *thought* I needed the money. The money's gone. The car's gone. Stupid, stupid, stupid. Sometimes a guy doesn't understand what he's got."

"I won't sell this one."

"Good." He began to walk back to the sign.

"Hey! Hey, Rabbi!" Hooter called as he dug into his wallet. He pulled out four hundred dollars.

"You don't need to do that," Goldberg said.

"For Jerusalem," Hooter said.

"Okay, then. You run into trouble, you call me." Goldberg was just about certain he hadn't seen the last of Hooter.

"Thanks," Hooter said. *God bless the Heebs*, he thought with the familiar vibration of the steering wheel in his hands. *God bless 'em.*

chapter **Sixteen**

The clarinet player was sucking on a reed, sitting on a plastic red milk crate, when Hooter found him. The cardboard box at his feet had a new sign. Give Peace a Chance, it read.

"How's Maggie's?" the old man asked.

"It's a shithole," Hooter said. "There's a place a block farther down that looks nicer for the same price."

"Oh, it is," the man said. "Much nicer."

"Why didn't you tell me about that one?" Hooter scratched his head.

"Because it's too comfortable. People get too comfortable, and they never get busy doing what they ought to be doing. They end up on the street. They never leave. Maggie is the best motivator there is. No one stays there long."

In her own way, Maggie was making the world a better place, but Hooter didn't see it at the time.

"Yeah, but she has my money."

"How much you got left?"

"'Bout a hundred fifty or so."

"What! You a dope fiend, boy?"

"No." Hooter explained about the impounded car and the Heebs and the Jerusalem Fund.

"You shouldn't have given me half of your winnings," the old man said. "You want some of it back?"

"Nope. Fair is fair," Hooter said.

The old man nodded. Then, because he was tired of me referring to him as *the old man* or *the clarinet player*, he extended his hand.

"Name's Luxom DeShane. When you need *de* man to lend *de* hand, *de* man to call is DeShane." He chuckled at his own little joke, which he told to everyone. It didn't seem to matter that no one ever laughed along.

"Hooter Pridley," Hooter said, because that was his name.

"You're a good man, Hooter Pridley," Luxom said. He pulled a pen out of the box and tore off a corner of the sign. He scrawled a number and pointed to the pay phone ten steps away. "That's the only one that works in a square mile. That's how you can reach me. If you got questions about this nuthouse town, call."

Hooter raised his hand as if he were back in school. "I think I need a job."

"You play clarinet?"

"Nope."

"Can't help you on that one, then. See that news rack? Grab one of those *Job Hunter* papers. They're free. Complete waste to put them down here, if you ask me. Folks use them for blankets on the park benches. Or they burn them to keep warm at night. No one down here actually *wants* a job. You might be the first."

When he pulled that paper out of the stand and began searching for a job, Hooter felt a little like Neil Armstrong. There was a need for lots of work Hooter didn't know how to do and lots more work he didn't *want* to do. But all of it was better than going back to Maggie's Shithole.

One ad was bolder than the others and contained red print: "Wanted Immediately! Maintenance Engineer. Knowledge of heating and cooling systems a plus. Five hundred dollars a week. Benefits, including dental. Apply at Horowitz Medical Plaza." The address was in Burbank.

There wasn't much Hooter couldn't fix. His father was a janitor, and Hooter knew that's what a maintenance engineer was. Hooter was the one who did minor wiring and furnace tweaks at Wangdoodle Auto & Truck Parts, and it had saved Peter Wangdoodle a wad of cash over the years. Once, Hooter had repaired the main air compressor for three dollars in parts. That was after the company rep told them the whole thing would have to be replaced.

If the world was a jumbled, confusing, unorganized mess in Hooter's eyes, machines were not. They made perfect sense and were utterly predictable. If they acted unpredictably, it was only because you did not understand them well enough.

People were impossible. Especially women. They were ethereal. Changeable. Magical and evil spirits all in one. If he could have accepted that, it might have been easier for Hooter.

Weird stuff happens. You move on.

People flake out. You move on.

But Hooter kept trying to figure them out. People were machines of a sort, he reasoned. Predictable, if you understood them well enough. That's what he had come to admire about Freud and Jung. They had actually attempted to define the machinery. They had only succeeded in revealing their own inconsistencies, as far as Hooter could see. But they had tried. He admired them for that.

But enough. On to Burbank.

chapter *Seventeen*

Hooter was nearly bowled over by an angry man at the entrance of Horowitz Medical Plaza. The man was followed by a woman in a pink suit mincing along on high heels.

"Dr. Van Horn! Dr. Van Horn! What about your appointments?"

"Let Horowitz figure it out! Maybe my slut wife can help him!" Van Horn spat. He slammed the door to a silver Porsche and, with tires burning, roared out of the parking lot, clipping the curb as he left.

The woman in pink smoothed her suit and walked to the receptionist at the switchboard, who put a caller on hold. "Cancel all of Dr. Van Horn's appointments."

"Today's?" the receptionist asked.

"All of them. Forever. Tell them we'll do our best to reschedule within the office."

When the woman left, Hooter rose to approach the receptionist. Her identification tag said Wilma.

She waved him off as she resumed a hushed conversation on the phone. "Look, I gotta go ... *Just now!* Left like he was on fire ... Yes, walked right in on them. The buzz is Horowitz's wife is talking divorce. Plus, Horowitz is out five hundred dollars an hour for every canceled appointment ... *I can't.* Got to go. Yeah. *Yeah.* Bye."

The receptionist smiled at Hooter. "May I help you, sir?"

"I'm here to see Dr. Horowitz."

"Do you have an appointment?"

"No, ma'am. It's about the opening. Maintenance engineer."

"I'm sorry. I don't know anything about that. I'm just a temp. There's a … little *reorganization* going on here today. Have a seat. I'll ring his office and see what I can do."

Hooter walked back across the marble tile and settled into a black leather couch. He counted twelve doctors on the brass directory on the wall. Horowitz and the defunct Van Horn were psychologists. There were couples counselors, plastic surgeons, dentists, acupuncturists, herbologists, podiatrists, and hair-replacement specialists.

"Sir?" the receptionist called.

Hooter rose.

"I'm so sorry. The position was filled. Yesterday."

Hooter's head drooped. He shuffled toward the door. "Thanks."

The phone rang. "Hi. Yeah. In the *coat closet*. Yup. Red-handed. Yup. Quit. No, it's my last day … Maternity leave … She's back tomorrow."

A dejected Hooter shambled back to his car. As he drove the tony streets of Burbank, Hooter Pridley felt farther away from the warm embrace of Trixie Foxalot than ever. He needed money. He needed prestige. After topping off the gas tank, he had just a little bit more than a hundred dollars. And he had five nights left at a shithouse named Maggie's before life really got hard.

It was at that moment, as he wove through traffic near the freeway, that he spotted the massive billboard. Another sign from God. Trixie Foxalot looked disheveled and sweaty. She was wearing pink spandex, and her cleavage was a good four feet long. She stared out at Hooter with heavy-lidded eyes and pouty lips. "Adonis Muscle Center knows how to handle my body" the billboard read. There was a phone number: 555-5555. As he motored, Hooter scrambled for a pen and paper but found none. He would be forced to memorize the number.

He wheeled alongside the first phone he could find and dropped a quarter into the slot. "I'd like to speak to Trixie Foxalot," he said.

"Just a moment, please."

Just a moment, please! That was promising.

"Excuse me, but Miss Foxalot is on the Stairmaster. She wishes to know who is calling, please."

Who's calling? Who's calling! Hooter hadn't thought that far ahead. He couldn't very well just say Hooter Pridley and have her know instantly that the love of her life was on the line.

"Sir?" the voice on the line asked impatiently.

"Uh, Pridley. *Doctor* Pridley."

There was a click and a minute of music by Yanni.

"I'm sorry, Dr. Pridley, but Miss Foxalot cannot come to the phone at the moment. Another time, perhaps."

"Sure. But one more thing. How much is a membership?"

"Five hundred dollars ... "

"Fine."

"... a week."

Gulp.

"We accept credit cards. Shall we sign you up now? We're running a special. You get one-on-one buttocks-tightening instruction free."

"I'll think it over."

Five hundred dollars a week. Even if he had gotten the janitor job, Hooter couldn't have afforded an Adonis Muscle Center membership. It was only midmorning, but he was already exhausted from the rising of hope and the smack of reality.

You can see how easy it would be to flit from highs to lows in the City of Angels. It would kill you after a while if you got emotionally involved with all the soaring and plummeting. That explains the jaded, disaffected tone of the people. Deep down inside, they want to care. They *do* care. But even those who touch the stars invariably pull back, scorched and disillusioned.

Apathy becomes the appropriate response to every situation.

chapter *Eighteen*

It was desperation that hatched the plan.

Desperate men form desperate plans.

It was astonishing to see Van Horn speed away in a Porsche 911 from a job that had clearly made him a rich man. Hooter understood Van Horn's pride and anger. But still, consider the irony of it all—Hooter couldn't land a five-hundred-dollar-a-week job and Van Horn abandoned a job that made him five hundred before the first coffee break. If Hooter could be Van Horn for just a few months, his life might be transformed. Meanwhile, Van Horn couldn't even stand being Van Horn for another five minutes. Sometimes one man's hell is another man's heaven.

Hooter's mind whirled.

It was an audacious plan.

It could never work. Never in a million years could it work. But in his mind Hooter heard the voice of his father: "If you set your mind to it, you can do anything." But that wasn't what really motivated Hooter in that moment. It was the thought of going back to Maggie's Shithole. Say what you will about Maggie, but when it came to the motivational sciences, she could give Tony Robbins a pretty good run. Hooter had to act now, and decisively. He had the rest of the day to become a doctor. He stopped at the nearest library. At this point, he could not afford to buy books, and he had to cram for the biggest test of his life.

A mousy young woman with glasses and a striped sweater smiled at him as he stared at the daunting rows of books in the psychology section, wondering where to begin. Hooter smiled back wanly. She smiled some more and moved closer.

"Have you read the newest from Schlossenpfennig? It's turning the psychiatric community on its ear."

"No, I ... "

"You should read it, then. They say his *Theory of Abstraction* is a real breakthrough."

"Are you a shrink?"

"Heavens, no! I'm a patient. I'm obsessive-compulsive. When I have a breakdown or get sick, I have to study and read until I know everything there is to know about it. I could take your gallbladder out right now."

Hooter appreciated the offer, but decided against it, what with his rigorous timetable of becoming a doctor and all.

"For instance, last week my shrink diagnosed me as obsessive-compulsive, so I ran to the library to learn everything I could find out about being obsessive-compulsive."

It sounded counterproductive to Hooter, but he was too polite to say so. "Have you been a patient long?" he asked.

"Heavens no! It's a court order. There was a big to-do about it. They caught me fixing the modern art at the museum. I know *everything* there is to know about art. But modern art just never looks *finished* to me."

"So you finished it?"

"Yeah. I couldn't help myself. ... So what's your story?" she asked.

Hooter was about to tell her that he came from Sterling, Colorado, where there are no mountains, in a classic 1970 Barracuda. He could have mentioned Trixie Foxalot, the Rastafarians, the Mormon Goths, striking oil, and the dead Wayne Noodler. He could have mentioned Cyclops and the bald-headed clarinet player on Sunset Boulevard. He was about to tell her when the thought struck him—"If I tell you about me, there's a chance you could obsess about it, right?"

"It's what I do."

"You'll understand if I don't tell you, then?"

"Completely. I'd consider it a favor." She reached to the shelf behind him and pulled out *Theory of Abstraction* by Helmut Schlossenpfennig and handed it to him.

"Thanks," Hooter said. He noticed the hand that had handed him the book was still extended. He shook it.

"Molly McDonald."

"Hooter Pridley."

Hooter hefted the prodigious volume. Schlossenpfennig was a genius. It said so right there on the cover. There were accolades from men with stern-sounding names representing stern-sounding colleges and institutes. Hooter pored over the book. Even the summation was overwhelming. The man's mind seemed to run in circles.

"Excuse me," he said to Molly, "does anybody get this?"

"I didn't. And I have an IQ over two hundred."

"These professors all seem to love it," Hooter said.

"Yeah, but ... What if none of them get it, and they're all afraid to seem stupid, so they just call him a genius? Then anyone who reads it will automatically assume they're just not intelligent enough to understand it."

"Wow. That could make your head spin just thinking about it."

"It does," Molly assured him. "Psychology is like modern art. Everyone has too much pride to admit they don't understand it. I didn't want to admit that I didn't understand Schlossenpfennig until you did. ... You know what's funny?"

"What?"

"Psychiatrists are always coming up with ways to manipulate people. Like, for instance, if they ask you if you're an alcoholic and you say no, they say you're *in denial*. And denial is a sign of alcoholism. Everyone's nuts by those convoluted standards. It's one mad circle. I think Schlossenpfennig has got them going in one big circle and no one knows it. Except you and me."

"Wow."

"And maybe Schlossenpfennig. In which case, he *is* a genius."

There was a whole row of books on Schlossenpfennig, all debating the levels of his brilliance and his revolutionary importance to the study and healing of the human mind. There were some biographies, all unauthorized. The man, it seems, was a recluse. He lived in Chicago. He refused to be photographed. No one seemed to know him except by his work. He sounded half nuts.

• • •

Hooter copied the resumes of various psychologists. With thirty dollars, at a print shop that otherwise specialized in pornography, Hooter was able to procure diplomas from several colleges. He also had a resume and a letter of recommendation printed up from the great Helmut Schlossenpfennig. The man at the computer did not seem surprised by these requests. He helped Hooter pick diplomas with gold embossed foil.

"Need a passport?" the man asked. "Green card? Social Security card? ID?"

"I don't think so," Hooter said.

"You licensed to practice psychology in the State of California?"

"No."

The man spooled through some files and pecked at the

keys. The printer whirred. "You are now. Congratulations, Dr. Pridley."

A supervisor walked up from the back as Hooter was walking out. "Fake ID?" he asked.

"Headshrinker credentials."

"Okay. But no more gynecologists."

"Right."

"I mean it."

• • •

It took another twenty-four dollars at the Salvation Army Thrift Shop for Hooter to get a houndstooth jacket with patches on the sleeves and trousers to match. The shoes pinched, and the belt was plastic, but a good quality plastic. He got a pair of round glasses, with a weak prescription, that slid down his nose. He looked older when he checked himself in the mirror. Slightly rumpled. The glasses gave his vacancy a more thoughtful appearance.

He studied his resume all night. It was covered in the medicinal-smelling flea-and-tick powder the boys at Maggie's were passing around. He tried hard to remember the theories of Jung and Freud and a bit of the genius of Schlossenpfennig, until it was all an impossible, tangled jumble in his mind.

By ten, he was in a panic.

Then he remembered his old granddad and what he had said after the funeral of a lifelong friend. They had been cowpokes together as youths, best men at each other's weddings, and often lent a hand to one another on big tasks.

Hooter's grandfather was there the day they buried his friend's wife. Shortly thereafter, the man took to drinking, and although they had ridden and worked together in near silence for forty years, the man began to pour his heart out to his friend.

"I never knowed what a fool he was until he started talkin'," Grandpa Pridley said.

By then, it was too late. He had to stick by the man for another six or seven years, until the booze mercifully cut short the torment for them both.

Hooter considered the memory and resolved to say as little as possible to Dr. Benjamin Horowitz. After that, Hooter Pridley, *Doctor* Hooter Pridley, slept like a babe.

chapter Nineteen

Doctor Hooter Pridley strode confidently to the front desk of Horowitz Medical Plaza. The receptionist desk was a model of efficiency. Wilma, the temp, had been replaced by the regular receptionist. Although it was her first day back from maternity leave, she hadn't missed a beat.

"Good morning, sir. How may I help you?"

"I'm Dr. Pridley. I have a ten o'clock to see Dr. Horowitz."

She ran her finger through the appointment book. "I'm sorry, Dr. Pridley. I have no record of an appointment and ... "

"I confirmed it yesterday by phone. I *flew in* from Chicago this morning."

"Oh, my." She buzzed Horowitz's secretary and explained the situation. As she listened, she covered the bottom of the phone and spoke to Hooter. "Dr. Horowitz is booked for weeks. We're shorthanded ... "

"Tell Horowitz that's why I'm here. What kind of outfit is this? A man flies in from Chicago for an interview and there's no record of it? This does not appear to be the kind of facility I want to work for!" He started to stomp off.

"Dr. Pridley! *Dr. Pridley!* Just a moment. I'll see what I can do. I am so sorry. It's my first day back. We had a temp service. They're usually very good ... "

She was interrupted by the voice on the phone. She turned away and cupped a hand around the mouthpiece and growled into it. "I don't care if you have to bounce *two* schizos. You guys messed it up. You fix it!"

She listened to the voice, nodded, and smiled. "Will ten-fifteen work for you, Dr. Pridley?"

"That will be fine, I guess."

"You'll be more comfortable in Dr. Horowitz's waiting room. Fourth floor."

Horowitz's secretary was in the midst on an apology to a man who looked familiar to Hooter. He recognized the man as he walked out. He was a game-show host.

The apologies began anew. "Oh, Dr. Pridley. I'm very sorry about the mix-up."

"These things happen," Hooter said.

She beamed. He seemed quite civil, after all. "Coffee, Dr. Pridley?"

"That would be nice. Thanks."

A few minutes later another familiar face emerged from the polished ebony door to Horowitz's office. Hooter remembered her from a sitcom that involved an alien puppet. When she was gone, the secretary announced his presence into the phone.

"You may go in, now," she told Hooter.

"Dr. Pridley!" Horowitz said. He extended a manicured hand. "A pleasure."

"Same here." Hooter handed him the resume and the letter of recommendation.

Horowitz sank into his chair behind the desk. Without looking up, he waved Hooter to a chair. "Impressive. *Very impressive*. But one thing puzzles me. How did you know there was an opening? We haven't even sought resumes."

"I have my sources," Hooter said.

"Indeed. A man with these accomplishments no doubt has sources."

When he got to the letter from Schlossenpfennig, Horowitz gave a small involuntary gasp. He quickly recovered. "So you were mentored by Helmut Schlossenpfennig?"

Hooter nodded nonchalantly.

Horowitz continued. "Dr. Pridley, please forgive me, but I have to ask. And don't get me wrong. We have *exclusive* clients with *exclusive* psychoses … " He chuckled at his little joke.

Hooter smiled.

"But my dear Dr. Pridley, surely you are utterly over-qualified for the position."

Hooter could feel it slipping away. He had put together such an impressive resume, he had intimidated Horowitz.

Horowitz also wondered if this Pridley was some sort of star chaser.

"Honest work is honest work," Hooter said, quoting his grandfather, but he could see that Horowitz was still suspicious, so he gambled. "But the truth is, Schlossenpfennig recommended you. He's been following your work. He's impressed. I'm here to *learn.*"

At this, Horowitz blushed. He simply could not help himself. He stammered, "I had no idea … I mean, there have been papers published … and some small accolades. But I had no idea a man like—"

"He's *very* impressed," Hooter said when he probably should have shut up.

The most surprising thing about the meeting was that Benjamin Horowitz did not float out of his chair. Moments before, his life was chaos. His wife had left him. Van Horn had quit. The patients were in an uproar. If he did not replace Van Horn with the right man, the patients would follow Van Horn to another practice. The business end of Horowitz Medical Plaza could be a shambles in weeks. All those worries covered Horowitz like a shroud, and just when his life was darkest, a ray of light! A message from a god—a genius. The great Helmut Schlossenpfennig.

Horowitz studied the letter as if it were something sacred. *Breathe! Breathe!* Slowly he steadied himself. He *must* talk to the great man. It would be under the guise of getting a more substantial reference, of course, but perhaps in the course of the conversation Schlossenpfennig would discuss Horowitz's own work. It would be a blessing from a god.

It would kill Van Horn.

Van Horn was never able to completely hide his disdain for Horowitz's limited abilities. Perhaps that was why Horowitz seduced the young Mrs. Van Horn—a subconscious need to retaliate, to assert his dominance. But Horowitz didn't want to think about that. He was already dreaming of a meeting with Helmut Schlossenpfennig, Master of the Mind. But there was no phone number. He searched the stationery top to bottom almost frantically.

"Is there a problem?" Hooter asked.

Horowitz spoke casually. "I'll need a bit more information from Dr. Schlossenpfennig. You understand. It's procedure."

"Of course." Hooter wondered if the pounding of his heart was visible.

Horowitz didn't notice. To be so close to greatness ... he must not appear overeager. "I don't see a number," he said.

Hooter was ready for that one. "The doctor does not take phone calls."

"Perhaps since the doctor is an admirer of mine, he will make an exception."

"Perhaps," Hooter said. *Damn! Damn! Damn!* He was cornered. He reluctantly reached into his wallet and pulled out the scrap of paper bearing the number of the only working phone booth near Maggie's Shithole. That is how Dr. Benjamin Horowitz came to receive the number of a bald-headed clarinet player on Sunset Boulevard.

Horowitz smiled as Hooter penciled out the number on a notepad. Then he frowned. "This is a local exchange."

"Yes. Uh, Dr. Schlossenpfennig came along. Uh, he

wanted to see the Dodgers play. He's a big fan from way back. He's at the hotel."

"Marvelous!" This was new information. No biography on Schlossenpfennig had *ever* mentioned baseball. Horowitz wondered if Mr. Smarty Pants Van Horn knew *that*! "This is perfect. I have an executive suite at the park. I'll make the arrangements."

"Well, uh, that's awful nice. But, uh, Schlossenpfennig only goes to games alone. He doesn't like interruptions. He won't even take me."

"Pity."

"Yup. Pity."

"So which hotel are you staying at? Perhaps I'll just drop by."

"I wouldn't do *that*," Hooter said. By now, his collar was soaked. "One of his best friends did *that* … ," Horowitz sat back in alarm, "… and all I can tell you is, they're not friends no more. *Any*more."

"I've heard he guards his privacy."

"Big time."

"Just a call, then."

"Just that." Hooter checked his watch. "But don't chance it until after three. He sleeps late."

That seemed to satisfy Horowitz. He eased back in his chair, lightly drumming his fingers. "So tell me. What's Schlossenpfennig like?"

"He's kind of a hard person to get to know."

"Hmm. So they say. What about his Theory of Abstraction?"

"Personally, I don't know what all the fuss is about," Hooter confided.

"*Really?!*" That's what Horowitz had thought. He hadn't a clue what it all meant, and he had read the thing twice.

"Yeah," Hooter said. "Everyone acts like it's so confusing. It's pretty basic, if you ask me."

Horowitz blanched and deflated. That's what Van Horn had said. "Of course," Horowitz said.

Hooter rose to leave.

"I feel very good about this meeting," Horowitz said. "I have the feeling we'll be able to come to an agreement. Where can I reach you?"

"Same number," Hooter said.

Horowitz went green. The man before him was sharing a suite with a legend, and he acted as if it was just another day.

chapter Twenty

Thank God, Jesus, Mother Mary, and all the saints, Luxom DeShane was on duty. Hooter roared up, got out of his car, and ran so frantically toward the old man, he frightened two Japanese tourists away.

"Easy, boy! You're killing business!"

Breathlessly, Hooter explained the predicament.

When he was done, Luxom put his arm around him. His eyes squinted mischievously. "You got a bit o' grifter in you, boy. I woulda never guessed. Reminds me of the old days. Yeah, I'll help you. I'll take the call."

Three o' clock passed. And three-thirty.

Back at his office, Horowitz was in a dither. This was a huge moment. *Huge!* If he blew it, it might ruin him. But he had to call, he knew it. In five minutes—five more minutes to compose himself. Then he would call.

Meanwhile, tension rose at the pay phone.

"I'm out of here," said the bag lady whom Luxom had hired to play the hotel receptionist. She already had her ten dollars, she figured.

"Stay," Hooter implored.

"I'm supposed to stand here all day for ten dollars? I don't think so!" She began to push her cart away. The wheels had not made two revolutions when the phone rang.

"Answer it!" Hooter said.

She stood with her hands on her hips. Luxom shook his fist.

She sighed and picked up. "Imperial Palace. How may I direct your call?"

"I'd like to be connected to the room of Helmut Schlossenpfennig."

"I'm sorry, sir. It says here he is accepting no calls."

Hooter began pacing. Luxom smiled. She was playing it perfectly.

But trouble was approaching. Hooter could see it.

It was 4:10 when the 4:10 bus pulled up, on time for the first time in a month.

"Please. This is an emergency," Horowitz said. Then he heard a deafening rumble and the hotel operator was drowned out. "*Hello? Hello?*" he yelled.

The bag lady began hollering back into the receiver. "*Hello? Hello?*"

Hooter covered his eyes. His life, Trixie Foxalot—*everything* was riding on a screaming bag lady with a crooked wig who was lost somewhere in the jumble of passengers unloading from the bus.

"What *is* that noise?" Horowitz asked as the door pneumatically whooshed shut and the bus mercifully roared away.

"I'm sorry, sir. It's the workmen. We're remodeling the lobby. Isn't it awful?"

Hooter uncovered his eyes. She was brilliant.

"I'll ring Dr. Schlossenpfennig's room," she said. "No one could possibly be sleeping with this racket, anyway. Please hold the line." She held the phone to her chest and rubbed her fingers together for more cash.

Luxom shook his head. It was robbery! The bag lady returned to the phone. "I'm sorry, sir. No answer. Shall I continue to let it ring?"

Hooter waved frantically. *Yes! Yes! Let it ring!*

Luxom wrestled the phone away. *"Who dares call me?!"* he shouted in a German accent so shrill, a startled Horowitz nearly dropped the phone on the other end.

"Excuse me. Dr. Schlossenpfennig?"

"Of course it is! Who else would it be? You vant to play twenty questions?"

"No, no. This is Dr. Horowitz. Dr. Benjamin Horowitz ... "

"Yes. But uff course."

Horowitz was relieved. The tone was almost civil. "Dr. Schlossenpfennig, I'm calling about an application I have from a protégé of yours, Doctor Pridley."

"He isss a geniusss!"

Hooter's chest puffed. He was, wasn't he?

"Do you mind telling me a bit about his work habits?" Horowitz asked.

"Oh, he's a vorker, zat one. Night ant day, he vorks. Day ant night ... "

Hooter waved him off frantically. Who wants to work *that* hard?

"But he needs his time off to be at his best," Luxom corrected. "You must insist. Promise me! Or he vill vork himself to a frazzle. You take care of ze boy. Plenty of vacation time."

"I promise!" Horowitz said. "You can count on me!" And in spite of himself, he saluted the phone. Only then did he realize that he had, in essence, hired Hooter Pridley. It felt rushed, but he wasn't about to cross Dr. Helmut Schlossenpfennig, Master of the Mind.

"Well, uh, thank you for your valuable time. There's just one—"

"*Vat?*"

Again, Horowitz almost dropped the phone. "Sir, I understand you're a Dodgers fan. It would be a huge honor if you would join me—"

"*Nein!* Baseball is like a religion to me! Ant I alvays pray alone!"

"Certainly. I—I can respect that. Perhaps dinner, then. My treat."

"*Dinner?*" Luxom repeated. He could not remember the last time he had eaten something he had not liberated from a trash bin.

Hooter began to wave again like a traffic cop.

"Where?" Luxom asked, intrigued. Hooter began jumping and waving in opposition. The bag lady thought he was doing jumping jacks.

"Spago?" Horowitz ventured.

"Spago? Vell, I suppose a man hass to eat." Luxom sniffed almost contemptuously.

Hooter felt woozy.

"How does eight sound?" Horowitz said. "Shall I send a car for you?"

"*Nein!* No car! Ve vill meet you there! Now, if you are done with your blabbing, I vill get off zis infernal phone!"

Click.

Hooter's legs were rubber. "Are you crazy?"

"No. Just hungry," Luxom said. "And Spago has squab with a kumquat chutney that's out of this world."

Hooter fumed. As nice as colorful people like Luxom DeShane might be, they are not predictable. Here's a hint for you: when someone is described as *colorful*, it means unpredictable.

• • •

Of course, Luxom would need a costume, and Hooter had just a few dollars left. But with the lure of dinner at fabulous Spago, Luxom didn't mind using his own money to shop the Salvation Army Thrift Shop. He insisted on a monocle and ended up buying a suit Basil Rathborne might wear.

He bought a walking stick with a brass cobra handle to round out the ensemble.

Through it all, Hooter sulked. *Spago?* It would be a disaster.

"Relax," Luxom said. "What's the worst that could happen?"

chapter Twenty-One

They were thirty-five minutes late. Luxom insisted on it. It seemed like something Helmut Schlossenpfennig would do. Horowitz was there half an hour early, so by the time Doctors Schlossenpfennig and Pridley arrived, he was drumming his fingers, drinking nervously. The waiters had begun placing bets on when or *if* Horowitz's guests would arrive. The pastry chef won fifty dollars.

Luxom waited like a debutante for Hooter to open the car door. He tipped the valet and strode into Spago imperiously, clicking his cane and squinting through the monocle as if he were marching to "Hail to the Chief." He surveyed the room as a lord over his land, gazing out over the lesser intellects.

Horowitz rushed from his seat to shake the great man's hand. "Sir, it is an honor to meet you!"

Luxom gripped the hand limply in disdain. "Of course it iss!" He stepped to the table and sat in Horowitz's spot.

Horowitz bit his lip. He *always* sat with his back to the wall. *Always.* He had a phobia about being shot in the back. He slugged another glass of Merlot and feigned composure.

When the waiter arrived, the Master of the Mind ordered so exquisitely and so abundantly, even the waiter gasped at the mounting bill. Horowitz silently added it in his mind.

Hooter ordered Alaskan king crab because he remembered Gladys Neidermeyer describing it as a culinary pinnacle. "You have *got* to try it sometime," she said. But when the crab was served, steaming and looking like alien spiders, he stared. He had no idea how to eat them. So he fiddled with his silverware uncomfortably as Horowitz and Luxom ate lustily.

The concerned waiter appeared at Hooter's side and nodded at the plate of amputations. "Is everything all right, sir?"

Hooter was at a loss. He couldn't very well confess that he had no idea how to eat them. The great Helmut Schlossenpfennig came to the rescue. He waved his hand dramatically over Hooter's plate. "Zis will not do! The menu says Fresh King Crab! *Fresh!* Zis is unacceptable!"

"I assure you, sir, it was flown in—"

"*It iss unacceptable!* Vee prefer food from zis decade! Take it away! *Schnell!*"

Other diners stared at the table. Horowitz wanted to crawl under it. He slugged his third glass of wine and poured another from the bottle at the table.

The waiter smiled stiffly. "Perhaps something else from the menu—"

"Tuna," Hooter said. "Tuna fish sandwich."

The waiter stared. Horowitz dropped his fork.

"And some pickles and chips," Hooter said.

"Yes, sir." The waiter vanished.

The kitchen would be in an uproar. A tuna fish sandwich, indeed! Horowitz was convinced Wolfgang Puck himself would storm to the table to spit in their food.

Hooter was nonplussed. He buttered another slice of bread.

"Ze key to life is to have escargot at ze ballpark and peanut butter and jelly at state dinners," Schlossenpfennig said.

"So true," Horowitz said, though he was thoroughly confused by the analogy. He was now on his fourth—or was it the fifth?—glass of Merlot. He tried to engage the Master of the Mind in a discussion of the Theory of Abstraction, but was rebuffed by the curmudgeon.

"Who vants to talk shop?" his Master asked, waving him off as he devoured his rack of lamb.

Horowitz retreated but, emboldened by his next glass of wine, reengaged.

Schlossenpfennig appeared bored by his own genius. "It iss vat it iss. You read ze book. Vat else iss there to say?"

Horowitz was crestfallen, and Hooter began to feel a bit sorry for him, when Schlossenpfennig tossed Horowitz a lifeline in the next sentence.

"I vould much rather discuss *your* vork, Dr. Horowitz."

"Oh, it's nothing, really … ," Horowitz stammered. He blushed.

Hooter's tuna was excellent.

"I like a humble man," Schlossenpfennig said. "Zat vay, it is easy for him to understand the magnificence that is *I*!" He laughed at his own hubris until his face was red. "But I choke!"

This alarmed Horowitz, and he leapt up, pulled Schlossenpfennig from his chair, and began hugging him from behind. Schlossenpfennig's monocle fell into the chutney. All of this confused Hooter, who had been so engrossed in his baby dills, he looked up and wondered why Horowitz was attacking Schlossenpfennig.

"Stop! Enough!" Schlossenpfennig cried. "Vat are you doing?"

Horowitz released the man. He could feel his face reddening. "Uh, the Heimlich maneuver. You said you were choking … "

"Choking? Choking? I was making a *choke*. A funny! *Chay*-O-K-E. Choke! Get it?"

The other diners settled back into their chairs, and the low murmur of conversation resumed.

Good Lord! Horowitz had made a fool of himself in front of the greatest mind in psychology since Freud and Jung. He sank into his seat, drunk and defeated.

"But enough of my chokes," Schlossenpfennig said mercifully. "Tell me about your work."

"Well, I'm sure you haven't read it, but I had a piece in *Cranium Monthly* substantiating the Law of Contiguity," Horowitz said timidly.

"It vas brilliant!" The Master said. "A toast!"

"Really? You think so?" Horowitz was back. He raised his glass. "And there was another piece I did, for *Psych Illustrated*. On the statistical analysis method … "

"I read that!" Schlossenpfennig said after slugging down his glass of wine.

"You did?"

"Zat, *mien* friend, vas nonzense!"

Horowitz almost choked.

"But the Law of Contiguity—zat vas brilliant!" He could see Horowitz was still wounded, though. "Don't worry, old chum. Half the shrinks I meet wouldn't know statistical analysis if it hit them in the arse!"

Hooter wondered if he was the only one who noticed that Schlossenpfennig's accent had evolved from German into something quite British. The man could not hold his wine. Of course, Hooter was feeling a bit tipsy himself.

"I like you, Horowitz!" Schlossenpfennig said. When he drank, he loved everyone. He leaned over and threw his arm around him. "But I must be frank with you … "

Hooter desperately wished he wouldn't be frank. *Dear God, don't let him be frank …*

"At first, when my young protégé said he wished to leave my employ, I vas upset. But he begged me."

"Oh, I begged," Hooter said. He inhaled another glass of wine.

Schlossenpfennig continued. "Sure, I said, Horowitz is a *genius* and he knows his Law of Contiguity, but vill he take care of you, my young friend? I haff an obligation to see that a brilliant young mind such as Pridley's is properly molded."

Horowitz happily drifted away on a sea of Merlot. *He was a genius.* The great man had called him a *genius*! The rest didn't matter. He gloried in his ascension. The words that followed drifted away.

An awkward silence snapped Horowitz out of his reverie. He realized Schlossenpfennig was waiting for a response. But what was the question, exactly? It was bad habit, tuning people out. Horowitz got paid five hundred dollars an hour for not listening at all. He desperately rewound the conversation in his mind.

"Pridley will be like a son to me," he ventured. "I'm sure he will be a fine replacement for Dr. Van Horn."

"Van Horn!" Schlossenpfennig snorted. "A second-rater. No offense, but he is a pretender. You are fortunate to be rid of ze fool."

It was Horowitz's finest moment. Nothing could tarnish it.

Sure, it was a little embarrassing and odd that when Tommy Lasorda stopped by to say hello, Schlossenpfennig, a man to whom baseball was a religion, didn't seem to know who he was. That puzzled Horowitz for a moment, but the important thing, Horowitz gloated, is that *I am a genius* and Van Horn, that smug prick, is a *second-rater.*

A pretender. A fool.

Check, please!

chapter Twenty-Two

"I trust Dr. Schlossenpfennig enjoyed his meal," Horowitz said the next morning after Hooter arrived in his office.

The truth was, Luxom hadn't said much beyond a burp and a groan. He dozed on the way back, awakening only to direct Hooter to an obscure warehouse where he would sleep. He was still on the dodge from Ivan.

"Yes," Hooter said in reply to Horowitz's inquiry. He tried not to say too much, in accordance with his grandfather's mantra on silence.

"Tell me," Horowitz said, brazenly fishing now, "did he say anything else?"

"Nothing much ... "

Horowitz's face fell.

Hooter noticed. "Except that you were a genius, and he liked you—"

"*He liked me!*" Horowitz latched on to the crumb like a starving man.

"But that you should never call him," Hooter amended. *When would he learn to keep his mouth shut?* "Oh, boy, I can't count the times Schlossenpfennig liked someone and they called him and ruined everything. Some of the professor's best friends are people who never see him." Hooter could feel himself digging deeper, but he could not seem to stop digging.

"An unusual man," Horowitz said.

Hooter shrugged.

"Uh, yes. Well, so, Dr. Pridley, I'm sure you're eager to discuss your compensation package."

"Nah. I just want to know what I get paid."

"Of course. I like a man who is direct. I will pay you one hundred and fifty dollars per hour."

Hooter shrugged halfheartedly. He was a bit hungover.

The silence unnerved Horowitz.

"Of course, the office will absorb all expenses ... We do all the billing."

Hooter nodded impassively.

Horowitz took the silence as a no and continued to negotiate with himself. "And after six months we'll bump you up to two hundred an hour."

Hooter's blank stare was unnerving. Horowitz could take it no longer. "Excuse me, Dr. Pridley, I need to know what you're thinking."

"I was thinking that whores in Nevada get paid two hundred dollars," Hooter said distractedly.

"My God, man! I meant no offense." The last thing Horowitz needed was to insult the protégé of the great Helmut Schlossenpfennig, Master of the Mind. "All right! All right! Two-twenty-five an hour to start. A ten-thousand-dollar signing bonus. Two-fifty an hour after six months. Van Horn was here *five years* before he got that much. And we'll pay your secretary."

"Secretary?"

"Certainly. I have a file of resumes. I insist that they all have at least minor degrees in psychology. I find it helpful. Sometimes I wonder if my secretary knows more than I do. When correspondence is required, she knows every malady. All I have to do is sign the letter. I have a few candidates here who may be even more astute."

Hooter swallowed and took the handful of resumes. If he had a secretary who knew *anything* about psychology, she would expose him in a week. "That sure is nice of you, Dr. Horowitz … "

"Ben."

"That sure is nice, Dr. Ben."

"Just Ben."

"Okay, *Ben*. I'll sure look 'em over. But I have, ah, … "

"Other requirements?" Horowitz winked and drew an hourglass figure in the air with his hands.

"Yeah. Yeah. Other requirements … "

"I understand. I like the ladies myself. You'll need to move quickly. We have you assuming Van Horn's workload starting tomorrow."

"*Tomorrow?*"

"Yes. I understand this is moving very quickly, but may I be frank with you, Dr. Pridley? If we don't move quickly, we may lose all of Van Horn's patients. That would put me in an extremely tenuous situation."

"We wouldn't want that," Hooter said.

"No, indeed. I realize that doesn't give you enough time to get a secretary, so I'll arrange for a temp. We had a woman at the front desk while the regular was out on maternity leave. Wilma was fabulous. I'll have her in here first thing in the morning."

Hooter stopped breathing for a moment. *Wilma!* She would remember him as the janitorial applicant. "NO! Uh, I mean, uh … "

"Certainly you cannot operate without a secretary. It's only temporary. I insist."

"But I have someone in mind," Hooter blurted.

Horowitz studied the curiously palpitating Dr. Pridley. Clearly he had begun to adopt his mentor's eccentricities. "Fine. We'll push the first appointment back to ten. If you don't have someone first thing in the morning, we'll call Wilma."

And Hooter would call in sick—forever.

"Welcome aboard, Dr. Pridley. The paymaster will

cut you a check for your signing bonus," Horowitz said. "Many of our employees find it convenient to bank across the street. You'll need to be at the top of your game tomorrow, son," Horowitz grinned. "Your first hour is Zippy Nightshade, and he's got a list of psychoses longer than your arm."

Zippy Nightshade …

Did he say Zippy Nightshade?

Zippy Nightshade!

The thought set Hooter's mind reeling. Hooter had all his albums. There was *Death Is a Hound Dog*, *Disembowelments I Have Known*, and *Relax, It's Just Your Execution*. You want to talk about a genius. *There* was a genius. Hooter would find a secretary one way or another. And then he would meet Zippy Nightshade, the hard-rockingest son of a bitch there ever was.

The bag lady had been brilliant on the phone with Horowitz. With a little scrubbing, she would be a perfect secretary, Hooter decided.

• • •

Luxom DeShane nodded sadly when Hooter told him of his plan. "She would be perfect," Luxom said. "But she's in the hospital. Don't know if she's gonna make it. Word is Ivan busted her up pretty good."

"Ivan? Why?"

"I think he's snapped. Tryin' to run everyone off the street. He hasn't been the same since you took him for the two grand. His pride couldn't take it. Everybody out here is at least half-ass crazy. He's always been mean. Now he's flat-out dangerous. It's my fault. I should have never put you up to it."

Hooter suddenly had a stomachache. "Maybe we should get you off the street. I've got enough money to get a nice place … "

"No," Luxom said. "Once a man starts running, he can't stop. I don't want to run. And I'm too old to run. Don't worry, I can take care of myself." He began to play his clarinet, but his heart wasn't in it.

Hooter noticed a new sign in the box full of coins. All You Need Is Love, it said.

chapter Twenty-Three

Zippy Nightshade, Satan's Ghoul, was a car wreck. A ten-car pileup involving a truck hauling live chickens. He slurred. He trembled. He didn't even seem to notice that Hooter had taken the place of Van Horn. There were a good ten minutes of caterwauling before Hooter began to understand bits and pieces of the syntax.

Zippy had been going through a tough stretch. Album sales were down. He just wasn't offensive enough for today's discriminating listeners. He was twenty years removed from the glory years of Dark Tuesday, the band he recklessly fronted until he became bigger than the band.

Zippy had been on top for years, his popularity exploding after he bit the head off a chicken in Memphis. The fans loved it. Polite society was appalled. It was great being evil. In order to further outrage parents and appease his fans, he began biting the heads off increasingly larger animals onstage until an improperly sedated raccoon turned on him and nearly took off his nose. After that, to prove he hadn't lost his nerve, he took on a platypus. That was to honor his Australian fans—he was originally from Brisbane. With animal-rights protesters marching outside alongside the Christian Coalition, Zippy defiantly chewed most of the creature's head off, but before he was finished, he began gagging on fur and had to be rushed offstage.

Critics said later it seemed to improve his voice.

But he realized that night that somewhere along the line he had morphed from Satan's Ghoul to Everyone's Fool. In time, parents stopped protesting and started asking for autographs. No one bothered to organize record burnings anymore. He still appeared in the papers from time to time—Zippy always made good copy—but now he was a running gag, and he knew it.

It was big news when he opened a chain of restaurants intending to serve *live* food. But the Department of Health refused to budge. So Zippy relented and went to sushi. If it was not alive, it was at least raw.

They called the chain of restaurants Carcasses. The waiters dressed like serial killers, and the openings were huge, star-studded affairs, but it didn't last long. One by one, the restaurants floundered and closed, leaving a stack of unpaid bills. Who'd a thunk it?

Sitting before his hero, Hooter had tears in his eyes at his fall. Then the man stopped talking and began twitching and drooling. Horrified, Hooter ran for help. Horowitz was in the hall, waiting.

"I think Zippy Nightshade is dying in my office!" Hooter said.

Horowitz was bemused. "He always does that. For attention. Didn't you read the file?"

"Uh ..."

"Don't like to start with any preconceptions, huh?"

Hooter nodded.

"I admire that. But you'd better get back to him."

Zippy was fully recovered from his episode, and the litany of problems continued. There were the fucking bills. His fucking income was a fraction of what it fucking had been. Royalties were fucking miniscule. Zippy Nightshade, Satan's fucking Ghoul, faced bankruptcy. He would lose his fleet of thirty-eight fucking luxury vehicles. He would be fucking forced to live in a fucking smaller mansion. He would probably lose his fucking third wife, too. She was twenty-six, stunning, and had no intention of living in anything resembling fucking poverty.

"How many cars do you really need?" Hooter asked.

"Two, if my wife don't leave. If she does, one will do."

"So sell the rest," Hooter suggested.

This threw Zippy into another brief convulsion. No one had ever presumed to talk to him about reality. "What are you talking about?"

"Well," Hooter said, "my grandfather always said that folks who own a lot of things eventually find that the things start owning them."

Zippy stared. "But even then, I've got no money."

"So get back to work," Hooter said.

"No one wants to hear my fucking shit."

"People love your shit. *Death Throes* changed my life."

"Yeah. I get a lot of that. But what about my wife? She'll leave me if I sell everything."

"Well, if she does that, she doesn't love you. Who wants to be with someone who doesn't love you?"

Sometime during the hour, Zippy Nightshade stopped shaking. He took off his sunglasses for the first time in years. It was all very simple, he realized. The worst that could happen had already happened. "My life is a huge pile of shit!" he said. "So what am I trying to hang on to it for?"

Hooter had no clue. But the hour was up.

Horowitz was waiting outside the door. It was always great theater to watch Zippy Nightshade reeling out of psychoanalysis, looking worse than when he went in. But this time Zippy didn't cling to the door frame as he lurched out. He looked almost normal.

"The new guy's *fuckin' great!*" he said to Horowitz.

Hooter followed him out.

"You're great," Zippy repeated. "And your grandfather's a fucking genius."

Horowitz watched incredulously as Zippy strode confidently to the elevator. "What did you tell him?"

"Oh, just some commonsense sayings my grandpa told me. I've got lots of them."

"I've never seen such a transformation … "

Hooter puffed his chest.

"For God's sake, don't cure the man!" Horowitz said. "It'll kill the bottom line."

Hooter noticed that his secretary's desk was vacant. He could hear the water running in the washroom.

"We have to talk about that," Horowitz said, nodding at the empty chair. "There's been a problem. Look." He pointed to the large canvas on the wall. "That's a Jackson Pollock."

"Yeah?"

"She connected the dots," Horowitz said. "In Magic Marker. Van Horn paid one hundred thousand dollars for it years ago. It's worth ten times that, at least. Or it was."

Hooter studied it. "I think it looks better."

"You don't understand. Van Horn has the movers coming today to remove all his things. He'll be absolutely be livid—" He paused as the wheels turned. Horowitz smiled slyly. "On second thought, it doesn't look *that* bad, does it?"

Molly McDonald emerged from the washroom with bright red, freshly scrubbed hands and began recounting the paper clips.

"Molly," Hooter said, "give me the markers."

She surrendered three of them.

"Don't do that again."

"I won't. The rest of them are landscapes." She rose to wash her hands again after touching the markers. Horowitz raised an eyebrow.

• • •

Van Horn *was* livid. He shouted into the phone so loudly, Horowitz could hear him even when he held the receiver a foot from his ear, which he did. The tirade went on for a good five minutes. Horowitz smiled through it all. He did not bother to deny defacing the painting. In fact, he *relished* the fact that Van Horn thought he had done it. It made him feel dangerous.

The Jackson Pollock was replaced with a velvet Elvis. Hooter's patients agreed it was somehow profound, and Zippy Nightshade loved it.

chapter Twenty-Four

Albert Hammond said once that it never rains in California. But, man, it was pouring when Hooter walked out triumphantly after his first day as a doctor. He started for his bare new apartment but could not erase the vision of his friend Luxom DeShane standing alone in the rain. And anyway, a victory is not much of a victory if it cannot be shared. It had been a very good day, and not even the rain could ruin it.

Luxom was shivering under the eave of the building when Hooter sprinted from the curb with a package in his hands and pasted himself against the wall beside his friend. He placed the parcel in Luxom's arms. "For you."

It was a long raincoat with a fleece lining, and it fit perfectly.

"Looks good," Hooter said.

"You look pretty stylish yourself."

"Got a signing bonus, thanks to you. I could afford a few suits. Even bought a membership to Adonis Muscle Center so I can meet Trixie Foxalot."

Luxom smiled, but it was a wistful smile.

"The first day went real good except for the part where my secretary ruined a million-dollar painting. But I got to meet Zippy Nightshade."

"Zippy Nightshade, huh? I used to play a few of his tunes," Luxom said flatly. "But most of the folks who liked them never had any money to toss in the box, so I stopped."

Hooter studied his friend. He lacked his usual spark, and his eyes were red. "Somethin' wrong, Luxom?"

"Janet's dead."

"Who's Janet?"

"The bag lady."

The water gurgled past in the gutter and their eyes were drawn to it. It seemed that time had stopped except for the water rushing along. Neither of them knew quite what to say.

"I've got a new place in West Hollywood," Hooter said finally. "Nothing fancy, but it's clean. C'mon. Let's get out of the rain."

Luxom shook his head. "On a day like today, the rain seems like the place to be."

chapter Twenty-Five

Surveillance was the key. After several visits to Adonis Muscle Center, Hooter had Trixie Foxalot's schedule pegged. She arrived at four in the afternoon and stayed until six. All he needed to do was to revise his hours.

With Helmut Schlossenpfennig's admonition to grant ample free time to the young genius echoing in his ears, Horowitz let Hooter juggle his schedule for an early afternoon workout. Why not? Things were going swimmingly. Almost all of the patients who saw Dr. Pridley raved about his homespun homilies. They seemed to strike a chord in the artificiality of Hollywood.

Desmond Carson, a three-time Oscar nominee and a Golden Globe winner, spread the word that Hooter was some sort of genius. All the Hollywood insiders were well acquainted with Carson's rotating phobias. They made him incredibly difficult to work with. During filming of a picture about coal miners, he developed achluophobia—fear of darkness—so they went over budget on lighting. But critics hailed it as the least gloomy-looking mine picture ever.

Another time, during filming of a comedy, he developed a fear of Tony Randall. Lots of people have that one. But in the space of a month, under Hooter's care, he was down to four phobias: selenophobia, fear of the moon; alliumphobia, fear of garlic; fear of vampires, ironic, considering the garlic; and fear of cheese.

In dismissing the other phobias, Hooter cited one of his grandfather's famous sayings, *You're born to die*, the point being, if you accept that you're going to die, the method is really a secondary issue. It always rankled Hooter's grandfather to see his philosophy stolen and screen-printed on the back of Harley Davidson T-shirts, but what are you gonna do? Take Hell's Angels to court for copyright infringement?

• • •

At the fitness center Hooter carefully studied Trixie Foxalot's routine, which combined strength training with aerobic exercise. He started placing himself on the machines before she arrived, straining mightily when she got there, so he didn't look like a slacker.

She was more beautiful in person, if you can imagine that. Maybe it was the sweat and the motion that made her more erotic. Before, she had been just a picture, animated only in his imagination. Hooter's love for her grew as he watched her, even as she was surrounded by a line of heavily muscled suitors.

She seemed to notice him—that distant look in his blue eyes was attractive, even if the sweat socks pulled to his knees looked dorky. She even smiled at him, and he smiled back, but that was as far as he got. He was petrified. How does one approach a goddess? And so the game continued. And in the beginning, he was content just to be near her.

He was distracted one day at the bench press when he followed a muscle-bound five-foot man who compensated for his stature by building his body sideways. Hooter should have pulled at least a hundred pounds from the bar, but he was already on his back when he noticed her watching.

He couldn't very well get up and start pulling weights off. She would think he was a weenie.

He pushed until the veins popped in his neck and he grudgingly held the weight above it. He tried to bring the weight down slowly, but his arms weren't up to it. The bar plummeted and pinned him by the throat. He began kicking his feet wildly, and the thought raced through his head that he was going to asphyxiate within feet of Trixie Foxalot. Everything went gray for a moment.

When things began to come back into focus, he saw Trixie Foxalot leaning over him, her awesome cleavage inches from his face. The squat weight lifter stood on the other side.

"He's breathing," a low, scratchy baritone voice said. "You should have had a spotter."

It was weird. The weight lifter had spoken, but the beautiful Trixie Foxalot's lips seemed to move. He looked at those amazing eyes, the matted blond hair, and those plump lips that screamed to be kissed. He was so close, it was all he could do to resist leaping up.

Then her lips moved again. "Are you all right?"

Her voice sounded like a gravel truck.

In fact, she sounded a lot like Zippy Nightshade.

That's the way it goes. Love is blind, and occasionally deaf. Love does not question. Love is hopeful when hope is lying comatose in the gutter. Love is obtuse, trusting of thieves and rascals. Love sees drought and says, "At least it is not raining today." If Love sat around analyzing things, it would cease to exist. So for its own good, and for the good of us all, Love ignores its disabilities and plods forward to the next disappointment.

Trixie Foxalot never failed to notice Hooter after that. They smiled shyly at each other from across the sweating, grunting bodies. Several times Hooter worked up the courage to approach her, but each time, as if he could sense it, Rico Juarez, who Hooter took to be her boyfriend, appeared at her side. He had a cleft chin and black eyes. His body was perfectly sculpted. He had no hair on his back.

Trixie's eyes seemed to apologize to Hooter as she left with Rico, but he understood. Rico Juarez was almost a star. The only thing holding him back was his accent. It was so thick, all his lines were dubbed by less handsome men who did not sound like Pancho Villa. When they spoke to each other—Rico, in his high Latin accent, and Trixie, with the voice of a pro wrestler—there was something unsettling and surreal about it. Instinctively, they understood this, so they communicated mostly with poses and steamy looks they had learned in acting classes. In the silence, they were magnificent.

Meanwhile, Hooter continued to document his adventures.

Dear Hooter,

I did it. I finally met Trixie Foxalot. I was dying at the time, so there wasn't much time for chitchat. I think she and a short guy saved my life. The bad news is, she is dating Rico Juarez.

Sincerely,
Hooter

He couldn't seem to devise a plan to wrest her away from Rico Juarez. He had never even had a plan beyond simply finding Trixie Foxalot. So Hooter did what all Pridleys do at times like these—he pondered. When you get right down to it, pondering is nothing more than a race between man and fate. If a man comes up with a plan and acts, he forces fate.

If he is too slow, fate will force the issue.

chapter Twenty-Six

Molly McDonald always arrived early to sharpen more pencils. She had filled a drawer with them, and had nearly exhausted the office's supply. She had counted every paper clip in the entire building. There were 93,189 of them.

Horowitz listened to the complaints about the eccentric secretary and the unusual Dr. Pridley from other offices, but he dismissed them. Pridley had a gift. The stars loved him and his grandfather's homespun philosophy. Revenue was up. So if he wanted an obsessive-compulsive secretary, so be it. Besides, she had not defaced a painting since the first day, and Horowitz found her quite attractive, in a bookish sort of way. And she knew her psychology. Pridley seemed to enjoy testing her. He would recount the details of his session, and she would offer a diagnosis.

As Horowitz had feared, Zippy Nightshade had been cured. There were no more theatrical exits from the office. The up side was, he kept coming back to hear Hooter recite the things his grandfather had told him. Things like, "You can't just search for gold where the light's good." Zippy loved that one. He took it as a sign that he should return to his roots, playing the bars like in the old days. He ignored the snide remarks in the Hollywood columns about his financial difficulties. He sold the cars and the mansion, and, yes, his wife did leave him. But Zippy gathered up a handful of edgy young musicians and started rehearsing. Sometimes Zippy would appear unannounced on the stages of other bands and belt out a song. The word was, he sounded pretty damn good.

While Zippy's life had simplified, Hooter's web was becoming more complex. He rushed into his office one morning looking particularly flustered, like he had just run the high hurdles. Horowitz was chatting up Molly when he entered.

"You look like you've seen a ghost," Horowitz said.

"Uh, no. I'm fine … Say, what's with Wilma at the receptionist's desk? I thought the regular was back."

"Yeah. Me, too. But that's the way it is with new mothers. Sometimes they decide they need to be with the baby. Happens all the time."

"So when do we get a *new* receptionist?" Hooter asked.

"We don't. I hired Wilma full time. We won't find one sharper than her."

Sharp? She was a hawk, and Hooter was a cottontail. He had almost been caught. He had breezed through the door and then, when it was too late, spotted Wilma on the phone. Thank God she was looking down. When she glanced up, he had his back turned and was hustling—almost running—down the hallway. The charade could implode at any moment.

"We've got problems," he told Molly after Horowitz left.

"We could whack her," Molly offered helpfully. "I got obsessed with hit men once."

"Did you ever get obsessed with prison?"

"Good point."

Thus the whacking was tabled. They agreed that he might be able to sneak past Wilma for a while, but eventually she would recognize him as the janitorial applicant.

"Let me think on this," Molly said. "I'll come up with a plan. I'll stop by your place tonight and we can work it out.

Right now, you've got more immediate issues. Desmond Carson is in there. He's not making any sense at all."

"Don't tell me his phobias are back."

"Well, he's no longer afraid of cheese, but he's got a new one. And he says he thinks he killed a man."

"Killed a man?"

That wasn't exactly true. The man did not die, though he had lost an ear and had been run through during a sword-fight scene. It was supposed to be Desmond's triumphant return to the action movies that had made him a star, and he and his costar were spectacular, until Desmond realized he had a phobia about Mexicans and the choreography went awry. The stagehands gasped when Rico Juarez turned toward them spouting a fountain of blood from his stomach.

"Rico Juarez? Did you say Rico Juarez?" Hooter asked.

"Yes," Desmond sobbed. "I don't know what came over me."

That's fate for you. If you don't come up with a plan, fate will go out and do something awful. Hooter believed in destiny, but he wanted no part of a destiny that involved shish-kebabbed Mexicans. He was relieved when he found out that Rico would survive—after a long convalescence. His ear never looked quite the same, though, and his career never recovered from the interruption. He ended up on *Hollywood Squares.*

Desmond's film *Lustful Pirates of the High Seas* had a huge opening week because everyone wanted to see the impalement. But it tailed off sharply after that, and Desmond retreated to light comedies—none, though, with Mexicans or Tony Randall. Or cheese.

As disgusted as he was with fate's methods, Hooter understood that the opening was his. Trixie Foxalot's eyes met his when he walked into Adonis Muscle Center that afternoon. Her lips trembled, and her eyes welled up.

"I heard what happened," Hooter said. "I'm so sorry."

She collapsed into his arms, sobbing, her chest mashed gloriously against his. "I don't know how I can go on," she said.

"Do you want me to take you to him?" Hooter asked, acting noble.

"No, no," she said, and threw back her head, "he would want me to go on."

It reminded Hooter of Scarlett O'Hara, though Trixie seemed genuinely distraught. She stepped back onto the Stairmaster, her sobs making her breasts heave against the spandex. "I love him so much!" she said.

That hardly seemed promising. "Well, I, uh, guess I'll leave you now."

"Please don't leave me alone! Not tonight," she said, even though it was still light outside.

"Well, maybe we could have some coffee and something to eat."

"Sure," she said, "as long as you understand we can just be friends. But I don't even know your name … "

"Hooter. Dr. Hooter Pridley."

She smiled broadly. "Doctor?"

"Psychologist," Hooter said.

Even then she regretted the "just friends" proviso. She extended her hand and said, "I'm Trixie Foxalot."

"I know," he said.

She ate like a sparrow and smelled like a field of wildflowers. Hooter tried to engage her on the topic of world peace, because he wanted her to know that it was a real concern of his, too.

Mostly she smiled coyly and batted her eyes. "I think we ought to just nuke them all," she rasped after considerable prodding.

That was certainly a novel approach to world peace, Hooter thought. *You have to give her that.*

"Dessert?" the waitress asked.

"I couldn't," Trixie said, and so the waitress pulled a

pencil from her hair and totaled the ticket. It was just a little over nine dollars.

"Where would you like to go?" Hooter asked as they drove in the Barracuda.

"It's early," she said, "and I adore this car. Let's just cruise."

Hooter drove past Luxom DeShane's corner on Sunset Boulevard, but the spot was vacant. A block away Ivan was plucking pigeons five dollars at a time.

Trixie was lured by the thump of heavy metal bass coming from a grimy alley bar, and she insisted they stop. They ended up listening to a heavy metal band called Fury of the Spurned and drinking tequila shots. With each drink Trixie's body pressed closer to Hooter, and he was overcome with desire. While the band blasted through their second set, heads in the crowd turned to the door as a striking figure in black marched to the fore. Hooter and Trixie sat up, momentarily distracted from their lust.

The singer stepped aside for the stranger, who turned to the crowd and began to wail as the guitar and bass players thrashed about madly.

It was Zippy Nightshade.

He was nearly drowned out by the cheers. He sang about demons and evil and sin and death, and Hooter proudly thought this might be the defining moment of his life. He knew Zippy would not be raging into the microphone if not for him and his grandfather's advice. Here he was, with his boyhood idol before him and his dream girl beside him. Sterling, Colorado, seemed a lifetime away.

Zippy's set included two oldies, "Leper's Lament" and "Fatal Death by Dying," and two new tunes, "Lizards in My Frontal Lobe" and "Bleed Them Dry and Watch Them Die," which was a ballad. The crowd howled for more, but Zippy leapt from the stage, hair streaming behind him, and strode toward the door. Bodies pressed back to let the legend pass. His eyes were alive with a newfound passion.

Twenty feet from the door he spotted Hooter and pulled him to his feet with a studded-gloved hand. He embraced Hooter before the incredulous stares of the crowd and an awestruck Trixie Foxalot.

"I love you, man!" Zippy said, and then he waded out into the darkness. That's all it took for Trixie Foxalot. If Zippy Nightshade loved Hooter Pridley, what was stopping her?

Rico Juarez's heart stopped twice that night, but each time he was shocked back to life. Hooter never knew that, and if Trixie ever did, she didn't seem to care. She had met this incredible new man—a healer, no less—and he was a mentor to Satan's Ghoul.

"Do you want to go back for your car?" Hooter asked.

"No, I'm afraid I had one too many drinks," she said. She slid her hand to Hooter's inner thigh. "Maybe I'll fix breakfast in the morning. Have you got eggs?"

I'm not saying Hooter set a land-speed record in the Barracuda that night, but it was easily a record for West Hollywood.

He fumbled for the keys at the door, embarrassed at his clumsiness. Trixie found his nervousness appealing. Gently she cupped his chin. Her long white nails grazed his cheek as she turned his head, parted her amazing lips, and kissed him. Her tongue swirled into his mouth.

Then the door opened from the inside. "I *thought* I heard something," Molly McDonald said, peering over her glasses. "I was organizing the silverware drawer."

Trixie looked as if she had swallowed a toad. She spun on her heel. "Well, I never!"

"Trixie! It's not what you think!" Hooter shouted. "Let me drive you home. I can explain."

She was already in the stairwell. "I'll get a taxi," she snapped. "You cad!"

Hooter didn't know what a cad was exactly, but he assumed it was derogatory in nature. "Aw, Molly," he groaned.

"Didn't you remember we have work to do?" Molly asked.

"Yeah, now I do—but how did you get in?"

"I got obsessive about locks once," she explained. "There's nothing I can't pick. This was a snap. C'mon. I've been waiting. We need to give you a new look if you are going to fool Wilma. So what's your pleasure? You want red hair or black?"

• • •

The disguise worked. Wilma didn't recognize Hooter when he walked in the next morning with jet-black hair and an instant tan. His collar was flipped up, his hat flipped down, and he wore sunglasses the size of saucers.

"Who was that?" Wilma asked.

"Dr. Pridley," someone answered.

"Is he some sort of kook?"

"No, he's a genius."

Hooter didn't feel like a genius. He just felt empty inside. He had won and lost the love of his life in a little over three hours. It was efficient, to be sure, but not as emotionally satisfying as one might hope.

He wanted to blame Molly McDonald, but the fact was, Hooter *had* promised to discuss her plan that night. Trixie Foxalot had changed everything, and Hooter had just assumed Molly would go back home when she got tired of knocking. It was rude, but we're talking about Trixie Foxalot here, star of stage, screen, and calendar. Any guy would have done the same thing. That's the problem with guys.

There's a moral to the story, and it involves rudeness. "People are rude because they think it speeds things up," Grandpa Pridley said once, "but civility is the grease of civilization."

chapter Twenty-Seven

It's hard to be concerned about other people's problems when your own are weighing you down like cement sneakers. Each day started with Hooter playing the part of a fugitive to get past the curious and increasingly starstruck eyes of Wilma the receptionist. She seemed intent on talking to this genius everyone raved about. He was a rising star.

Hooter had not mustered the courage to go back to Adonis Muscle Center. Trixie Foxalot had been furious. A *cad*, she had called him. You have to be mad to call someone that.

At times like these, there had always been a friend to talk to back home. Sometimes it was his one-armed, no-legged brother, even if the topic always rotated around until they were talking about his opposition to war. Even Peter Wangdoodle had empathy when things took a turn for the worse. But mostly Hooter poured out his heart to his journal and Gladys Neidermeyer. He could not let himself recognize that the ache in his chest was there because he was missing her. He thought about calling Gladys, but the last time he had seen her she had bounced a dildo off his nose, which is how girls say, "You cad" in Sterling, Colorado. His journal couldn't slap him on the back and say, "Everything is going to be all right" the way a friend would, even if it was a complete and utter lie. A real friend will look you in the eye as you are gurgling and frothing blood and say, "It's just a flesh wound." A real friend will lie his ass off because it's for your own good.

Hooter desperately needed a friend, someone who would understand his heartache over Trixie Foxalot. His time with her had been the happiest three hours of his life. There was but one person in the whole city whom Hooter could talk to: Luxom DeShane.

These are the things Hooter began selfishly thinking about when he should have been concerned about his patients' problems. Take Drusilda Judicious, for instance. As a wealthy heiress to a loofah cartel, her life was complete misery—she had all those tax shelters to worry about. One year she actually had to pay taxes, and Van Horn had to see her three times a week to ease the trauma. And the servants were so bothersome. She could tell that they didn't really respect her. Her life was hell on Earth.

And now she was hearing voices.

"I knew a kid in fifth grade who got hit in the head with a bat and all of a sudden he could hear radio programs," Hooter said. "It had something to do with his fillings. He could listen to baseball games right in the classroom. What do your voices say?"

"It's just one voice. It's Nipsey Russell. He keeps rhyming everything."

"Well for the kid in fifth grade, it was Vin Scully. So that's different."

That just goes to show you that rich people have their problems too. Sure, some folks might be living in cardboard boxes in the rain, but at least they don't have Nipsey Russell in their heads …

Strike that. Actually, some of them *do* have Nipsey Russell in their heads.

Nipsey Russell must be stopped.

"Everything is going to be all right," Hooter assured Drusilda. Later he would consult Molly to make sure that was true. Drusilda was the last appointment of the afternoon.

Horowitz bumped into Hooter as he was leaving. "Off to the Muscle Center?"

"Yeah," Hooter lied.

"So, lots of hot chicks at the Muscle Center?" Horowitz asked.

"A few," Hooter said, "but they have bad attitudes."

Horowitz sighed. He didn't need any more of that. The divorce was getting ugly. He couldn't blame his wife. He hadn't seduced Van Horn's wife because he wasn't happy with his own marriage. He just wanted to screw Van Horn. Just figuratively. Now Horowitz was alone and desperate for companionship. He had trolled for hookers but hadn't had the courage to stop.

Molly McDonald fascinated him. The fact that she was obsessive-compulsive was almost a turn-on. Heck, his soon-to-be ex-wife was schizoid. Crazy people were always more interesting. Horowitz had had several serious relationships with sane women, but he always broke it off because they bored him.

In medical school he had been told that he almost required crisis in his life. That quality made him a decent shrink and a sharp businessman. Horowitz Medical Plaza was a lucrative enterprise. Van Horn, and now Hooter Pridley, were the lynchpins. Without star shrinks, there were no stars, and that was the reason most of the other doctors leased space in the building. Prestige—and the chance to practice podiatry on game-show hosts.

Alex Trebek had bunions.

But here they stood, Horowitz and Hooter, and it looked for all the world like they had the world by the tail. But they were lonely, living solitary lives in houses built of cards on shifting sand, and the wind was picking up.

Sorry. My metaphor key got stuck.

The point is, they had it bad.

To make matters worse, Hooter could not find Luxom DeShane. He drove past his corner several times. On one corner he saw Ivan, and Ivan saw him. He glared, but it was a smug glare that unsettled Hooter. The only other hustlers on the street were hookers. The juggler was gone and so was the pail drummer, whose act consisted of two pails—one to receive contributions while he bongoed away on the other. Still, no Luxom DeShane.

Hooter pulled over to talk to a streetwalker a block from Luxom's corner.

"Hey, baby."

"Hi. You see Luxom DeShane?"

"Luxom DeWho?"

"The clarinet player."

"Nah. Ivan pretty much cleared the street six blocks in either direction. After the bag lady, they didn't need no convincing."

Hooter couldn't imagine Luxom running without a fight. That concerned him. He got the vacant look in his eyes he always got when he was thinking—or when his mind really was vacant. "So why didn't Ivan chase you away?" he asked.

"Sunset Boulevard wouldn't be Sunset Boulevard without hookers. Tourists would never visit if it weren't for us. Ivan would have no one to hustle if we weren't here. We're the main attraction, darlin'."

If you look at it that way, hookers are a vital cog in the economy.

Hooter idly eyed her legs. She had thick ankles, but other wise was quite attractive. "You should go to Charming, Nevada," he said. "Girls there get two hundred dollars a flop."

Her jaw dropped. It sounded like Utopia. A hooker's Eden.

"You'd be the second-prettiest girl there," Hooter said. "Maybe third, if one of them has a wart removed." He meant it as a compliment.

"Yeah. Well, so how do I rank on the boulevard?"

"You're the prettiest. Definitely number one."

She smiled. That was enough for her. She never left the street.

But, I wonder, shouldn't one aspire to higher things than being the prettiest whore on the block?

Hooter poked around for hours before he finally found Luxom DeShane in the last place he looked. It's *always* the last place you look. What kind of fool keeps looking after he finds what he wants? Lots of people do just that, though. Guys will get a perfect wife and perfect kids and then go blow it all by getting caught with a fifty-dollar hooker with thick ankles on Sunset Boulevard.

But this is about Luxom DeShane.

Hooter crept through the darkened warehouse he had dropped Luxom at the night he played the part of the great Helmut Schlossenpfennig, Master of the Mind. Rubble was strewn inside the giant, empty building. The riveted, rusty braces holding the walls up made it seem to Hooter that he was walking through a giant, dried-out carcass. Water dripped from the rotted ceiling. A ribbon of sunshine shot down from a gash in the roof. Dust particles seemed to climb the fading light.

At first Hooter thought it was the building groaning, but he followed the sound to the body of Luxom DeShane. He was unconscious but still moaning. His head was a mass of welts. A ring of dried blood encircled his mouth.

"Luxom! Luxom! Can you hear me?" Hooter asked as he cradled the old man.

His eyes fluttered open weakly. "That you, Eldrick? I told you I'd come back. Now run, get your mama." Hooter realized that in his delirium, Luxom was speaking to some long-lost son.

"No, Luxom. It's Hooter! You know, *Hooter!*"

The eyes sharpened. "Hooter?"

"What happened to you?" Hooter asked, though he already knew the answer.

"Ivan," the old man gasped. "He ran off the drummer, too."

"He wasn't very good," Hooter said.

"No," Luxom gasped, "but he drummed hard."

Hooter eased Luxom to a sitting position. His face was sallow, his breathing thin. "We need to get you to the hospital."

"No! No hospital. Be better to take me straight to the cemetery."

"Luxom, you need a doctor."

"Boy, no. No one ever comes out. I've seen it for years. No one ever comes out alive. Promise me. No hospital."

Hooter swept his hand across his friend's brow. It was ice cold. "Okay," he said, "no hospital." He eased the groaning old man onto his shoulder and carried him across the rubble to the car. No hospital. But he had to do something.

The old man was dying.

chapter Twenty-Eight

With Luxom sprawled out on the backseat of the Barracuda, Hooter sprinted to the door and began pounding. There seemed to be pounding from inside, too, a swift whacking sound that mocked Hooter's slower, more furious pounding on the heavy wooden door.

Inside, with sweat soaking through his T-shirt, Rabbi Goldberg pounded out his frustrations on the speed bag.

Pow-pow-pow-pow-*pow!*

Stupid people.

Pow-pow-pow-pow-pow-*pow!*

Some days you just want to scream.

Boxing had saved him. And God. He gave them equal credit. Boxing saved him from his anger. He would have killed by now. He would be rotting behind prison walls. Of this, he was convinced.

When he was twelve, God led him to a stinking gym and a short, gruff man with cauliflower ears who had been a featherweight contender in the thirties. Kid Hoffman.

At first Goldberg flailed furiously at the bags.

"Whatcha mad at?" the Kid asked him.

"The world," Goldberg answered.

"The world's gonna kick your ass if you're all muscle and no brain."

"I can't stop being angry."

"No, but ain't you gonna get madder if the world keeps kicking your ass? Fight smart. Channel the anger to your brain."

This is what Goldberg learned from Kid Hoffman, who was no longer a kid. But he was no punch-drunk has-been. The skills of youth had left his brain unscrambled, even in his winter years. A pragmatist, he did not see sense in trying to kill fury. He just wanted to harness it.

Sometimes Goldberg forgot fury even existed within him. He fought with calculating, brutal efficiency. When he was head butted, he remained stoic. When he was rabbit-punched and hit below the belt, he remained stoic. Opportunity eventually arose. There was always an opening if he could find the patience to wait. Then, when it was there, and his thunderous left hook whistled toward an unsuspecting chin, in that instant before impact, his anger leapt to his fist.

Pow-pow-pow-pow-*pow!*

At first he thought the mighty thumps he heard were his, but when he paused to steady the speed bag, it came again. It sounded urgent. He ran to the door.

"Hooter … "

"Help me. He needs help … " And then he was gone, running to the car.

Goldberg followed, his hands still bound in dingy white tape. "Why didn't you take him to the hospital?" Goldberg asked as they carried Luxom inside.

"He won't go. He thinks he'll die there."

"He might die *here*."

The rabbi gently undressed the old man and probed for broken things. He woke him and made him take liquids. In time Luxom seemed more comfortable. The moaning subsided.

"I'll do what I can," Goldberg said. "No promises. … So what happened?"

"Ivan."

"The card shark?"

"You know him?" Hooter asked.

"He taunts me when I do my roadwork. He always tries to get me to play. To gamble. He tests me," Goldberg explained.

"I'm gonna get him," Hooter declared.

"Oh? How?"

"I dunno. I'm just gonna get him."

"Ivan's counting on that."

"What?"

"Your anger. It makes it easy for him to win. Don't do anything now. Ivan will expect it. Wise men wait for an opening. Go now. I'll take care of the old man."

"Luxom," Hooter said. "His name is Luxom." Somehow, it seemed important that Goldberg know his friend's name.

"Luxom," Goldberg repeated. "You stop by tomorrow. We'll see how it goes."

chapter Twenty-Nine

Hooter's focus wavered the next day. His preoccupation with Luxom DeShane's welfare muted his instincts and awareness. He got sloppy. Wilma caught him sneaking in the back entrance. She was part bloodhound, and determined to meet her first real live genius. He hadn't yet donned his hat and sunglasses when she came skipping toward him to personally hand him an invitation to a charity bowling tournament some of the doctors held each year to raise money for scurvy victims. Hooter hastily and crookedly threw on the hat and sunglasses and took the envelope.

"Do join us," Wilma said.

"Maybe."

"It's for a good cause. Do you have any idea how many people scurvy kills each year?"

Hooter didn't. If he had been reading this book, he would have known the answer: not many. Maybe one or two pirates a year, tops. But who wants to fight against a really tough disease? Who has time for it? Unless *you* get the disease. Then you make time. Overall, the strategy of fighting beatable diseases is a good one. You don't have to fight so hard, you get a winning record, and you get to run around chanting, "We're number one!"

As he took the tickets, Hooter idly wondered if anyone had started a foundation to fight facial warts on otherwise perfectly good hookers. That was a cause he could get behind.

"Thanks," he said, tucking the tickets into his shirt pocket.

Wilma leaned back, trying to peer up his sunglasses, and Hooter could tell she was trying to place his voice as he walked away.

"There's free fondue and everything," she said, as if bowling with podiatrists wasn't enough. They were offering hot cheese.

Hooter wondered how long it would be before Wilma remembered who he really was. He had the sense of being aboard a sinking ship.

To make matters worse, Molly introduced him to a new patient. Hooter had come highly recommended.

"But let's get down to business, shall we?" Winrod Lister said. "Time is money, and I have a lot of things to tell you about."

He started in with a long list of complaints ranging from the proliferation of nuclear weapons to hangnails. Winrod Lister was morose. Depressed. Suicidal. He droned. He moaned. He was the whiniest bastard Hooter had ever heard. It was a full-fledged bitch-o-rama. A cage match of complaining.

"I know what you're gonna say, Doc," he said, though Hooter hadn't managed to wedge a word in yet. "They *all* say it. They all want to give me a prescription for depression. But I say, *hell no!* HELL NO! You know why?"

Hooter had almost formed the *W* with his lips when the man ended the suspense.

"Because I don't want to lose my edge," he said.

"What do you do?" Hooter asked in his first full sentence of the hour.

"Motivational speaker," Winrod said. "And you know what? I feel better already. You're good. But isn't there something else you want to tell me before I go?"

Hooter looked puzzled.

"A saying," the man prodded, "from your grandpa. I heard you always recite one of your grandfather's sayings."

Criminy. What would Grandpa have to say about this creep? Hooter's mind was a blank, and as we have previously established, that was not unusual. "Uh … uh … "

"Geez, I can hardly wait." Winrod leaned forward.

"Uh … uh … It, uh—it takes a big dog to shit a hundred pounds," Hooter finally blurted.

Winrod sat back, frowning.

"Unless he does it a little at a time," Hooter amended.

Winrod appeared stunned. Even Grandpa Pridley would have admitted that it wasn't one of his better ones.

"Wow," Winrod said. "Can I use that?"

"Have at 'er," Hooter said.

The clock crept that day. Even the most astounding statements from the patients could not draw Hooter's thoughts from Luxom DeShane for long. It was a blessing when Desmond Carson, the last appointment of the day, canceled. He had developed an inexplicable fear of heights so severe, he could not stand. He had been unable to arrange for a gurney to get him to his appointment on time.

• • •

Hooter cursed traffic as he drove toward the synagogue.

"How's he doing?" Hooter asked the second he entered.

"I think he'll make it," Goldberg said, "but he's very upset. It's all I can do to keep him resting."

"Can I see him?"

"For a minute only."

Luxom's color was better. His wrinkles didn't seem so deep.

"He's moving fluids," Goldberg said. "He must have laid there a long time without water."

Luxom was sleeping when Hooter bent to kiss his forehead.

The eyes cracked open, and the mouth attempted a smile. "Hooter, my friend ..."

One shaky, scraped hand clutched Hooter's shoulder. Tears formed in Luxom's eyes. "Ivan ... "

"He can't hurt you here."

"He took it."

Goldberg and Hooter looked at each other.

"Took what?" Hooter asked.

"My clarinet." He began to shake. A gurgling cough rattled his chest.

"Don't worry," Hooter said, "I'll buy you a new one."

Luxom tried to smile again. "It can't be replaced," he wheezed. "Artie Shaw gave it to me."

"Enough talk," Goldberg said, pulling Hooter away. He gently stroked Luxom's head. "Rest. Hooter and I, we'll figure something out."

"Who's Artie Shaw?" Hooter asked when they were outside Luxom's room.

"Who is Artie Shaw? *Who is Artie Shaw!* My father— God rest his soul—worshipped Artie Shaw. He is a great musician," Goldberg said. "Come. Sit with me. I'll tell you. I have all of my father's old records. We'll play Artie Shaw."

So they sat and listened to scratchy records as Goldberg recited almost verbatim his father's testament to Artie Shaw. Hooter understood then that the clarinet was a connection to real greatness.

They listened some more, and Hooter said, "I think Luxom is better than Artie Shaw."

"I've heard Luxom play," Goldberg said, "and I think so too."

"When he gets well, I'm going to tell him that."

"What? And slay his hero? Not such a good idea. It would kill Luxom, too. And my father—God rest his soul—would roll over in his grave." Goldberg studied Hooter's puzzled face. "You see, way down deep inside, I think maybe Luxom knows he's better than Artie Shaw. But if you said it, it might break his heart. Because he feels a loyalty to him. And if Artie Shaw inspired Luxom to become a better musician, maybe that makes Shaw the greatest anyway."

"Is Artie Shaw still alive?" Hooter asked.

"Artie Shaw will never die."

In a vague sort of way, Hooter thought he understood.

"Now all of this is beginning to make sense," Goldberg said.

Hooter leaned in. "What?"

"Luxom is not so badly beaten," Goldberg said. "It's plenty bad, but that's not the main problem. When Ivan took the clarinet, he took Artie Shaw. That's what's killing Luxom DeShane."

Hooter stared at the wall. "Do you think Ivan knows that?"

"He knows."

Hooter's eyes narrowed.

"What is it?" Goldberg asked.

"I have a plan."

chapter Thirty

Patience is a virtue, but it was not a virtue Hooter Pridley was well acquainted with. He was a man of action. Rabbi Goldberg, on the other hand, was a reasoned man of action. A plan works best when the victim least expects it.

Goldberg insisted Hooter keep his distance from Sunset Boulevard and Ivan. Out of sight, out of mind.

"And don't park that orange machine in front of the synagogue."

They agreed that Ivan probably had no inkling of their connection—they were counting on it.

Goldberg scouted Ivan's table, which had been set up on Luxom's corner. He made it a point to jog past every other morning as Ivan fleeced the sheep.

Ivan never failed to try to lure him in. "Hey, Rabbi. Pick a card! God ain't gonna let you down."

Goldberg spotted the clarinet under the table. No doubt Ivan was prepared to taunt Luxom if the old man returned.

One day Goldberg pretended his curiosity had gotten the better of him. "How does it work?"

Ivan tossed the cards around, flashing the queen of hearts from time to time. "All you got to do is pick the lovely lady, and you win the bet."

Goldberg ventured a sweaty dollar from his pocket. "It's all I've got."

Ivan smiled with yellow teeth. "We'll pretend it's a thousand … two thousand bucks. Just to make us nervous."

The cards flew. Goldberg concentrated. "That one."

It was the queen.

"Oh, God is on your side! It's a good thing we weren't playing for more," Ivan said.

Goldberg ventured a ten-dollar bet the next day and won again.

"I never seen anything like it," Ivan said, smiling. "I think maybe I cannot let you play no more. I'll go broke at that rate."

"That hardly seems like good sportsmanship," Goldberg said.

That seemed to offend Ivan. "Okay, okay. One more time. But you better make it worth your while. After that, I'm done with you. You're too good. God is on your side!"

• • •

Waiting. Just waiting for the trap to spring was hard for Hooter. It reminded him of ice fishing with his grandfather. They sat in a shack and stared at circular holes drilled into the ice. There were shacks up and down the lake with cold men inside staring at circular holes, swigging schnapps from pint bottles.

His grandfather liked to go on Saturdays. That was the day Grandma vacuumed and cleaned their modest home with great fervor. Saturday was also a day Hooter's grandpa liked to take it easy in his later years. But he could not relax with all that work going on around him. It made him feel lazy. So he ice fished.

There was a small neighborhood of men on the ice. Some men were out there every day.

"You can tell a lot about a man's home life by the time he spends on the ice," Grandpa Pridley told Hooter.

These are the things Hooter thought about as he sprinted on the treadmills at Adonis Muscle Center. He had felt like a caged cat at his apartment. He wasn't ready to face Trixie Foxalot. He was still terribly wounded by that *cad* remark. But the need to burn off steam won out. Knowing her schedule like he did, he tried to work out on the opposite side of the facility. Now it seemed her schedule had changed, and she seemed to always be on a machine near him. When she turned toward him, he looked away. When he looked at her, she looked into the distance.

On the third day he looked at her, she smiled tentatively, and Hooter's heart began to sing.

He stepped off his machine and walked to her. "I'm sorry about the other night. I can explain. She's my secretary ... "

She placed her hand on his wrist. "You don't have to explain. I was such a fool."

Their lips met softly.

"Did you do this for me?" she asked.

"What?"

"The black hair. The tan. So you could look like Rico? Did you think that's what I liked?"

It hadn't dawned on him that his disguise had made him look like Rico Juarez's less-muscled brother. "Uhh ... "

She seemed pleased by the effort. "Silly boy. Don't ever change for me. I love you just the way you are."

Love? *Love!* She said *love*! It was unbelievable.

• • •

Making love to Trixie Foxalot was everything Hooter had imagined it would be. His body vibrated to her touch. She was impossibly slender, except for her breasts, which stood proudly immovable on her chest like the Alps. Her breasts were tan—she had no tan lines at all. She made little gasps beneath him to urge him on.

Trixie's arms flew backward and clutched the headboard. It reminded Hooter of Gladys Neidermeyer and the handcuffs. Then, for some reason, Hooter began to think about torque wrenches. Trixie arched her back, putting her breasts on glorious display. She began thrashing and making alarming whooping sounds. When she peaked, a guttural wail came from her throat, and Hooter had to open his eyes to make sure he wasn't making love to Zippy Nightshade. It sounded just like the scream from "Crypt of Torment." Afterward it nagged at him that he had orgasmed while thinking about Zippy Nightshade. It was troubling indeed.

"What's the matter, baby?" the most beautiful woman he had ever seen asked as she snuggled against him, stroking his thigh.

Hooter didn't want to tell her about Zippy Nightshade. "Just thinking," he said.

It turned out to be the right answer, because Trixie Foxalot admired intellectual men. His distant stare was what had attracted her in the first place. He looked thoughtful even when he was thinking about nothing at all.

To be truthful about the whole episode, Trixie had thought about Rico Juarez a couple times as Hooter made love to her. But it was Rico Juarez with a brain and without the accent. Dreamily she ran her hand the length of Hooter's body and let it rest on his chest. Slowly her breathing steadied, and Hooter began to doze off too.

He was awakened by charging elephants.

She snored.

chapter Thirty-One

The good rabbi prayed before he walked out onto the street. The plan was sinful, but inaction seemed even more sinful. If God would just smite Ivan himself, the whole thing would be settled.

"I was wondering if you would be back!" Ivan said as Goldberg approached.

Goldberg smiled uncomfortably.

"So what is the bet?" Ivan asked.

Goldberg rolled out a hundred-dollar bill.

"A hundred? That's all? Your last shot at glory, and you wager a measly hundred?"

"It's all I have!"

"Chicken scratch!" Ivan said.

"Except … "

"Except?" Ivan asked. "Except what?"

"I couldn't. I can't. It would be wrong," Goldberg said.

Ivan loved wrong. "Tell me," he said, lowering his voice conspiratorially.

"The Jerusalem Fund. If I bet a thousand and won, we would only be a thousand short."

"Or if you bet two thousand, you would have enough."

"If I won. Maybe you could just give me two-to-one odds on the thousand."

"Maybe the pigeons will start shitting cream cheese, eh? You've already beaten me two times straight. That I'm still willing to play is a gift." Ivan raised his palms to the heavens.

"Two thousand, then. God forgive me if I am wrong."

Ivan began weaving the Magic Betty shuffle. Goldberg's eyes followed intently. He made a great show of praying with his hands clasped after Ivan had finished. When he locked eyes with Ivan, he was smiling.

"Well, Rabbi? Which one is it? Whose side is God on today?"

Goldberg's hand hovered over the center card and then slid to his left. "This one."

Ivan's Adam's apple bobbed. Magic Betty had hit a losing streak. He stared hard at the rabbi. Had he been swindled or was God truly on the rabbi's side? Goldberg tried to remain humble. Slowly Ivan reached inside his coat and began retrieving money. His eyes never left Goldberg's downcast face. He laid the bills out on the table. When they added up to two thousand dollars, Goldberg reached for them.

Ivan covered the stack with his own hand and leaned into the rabbi's face. "Something smells," Ivan said, "like fish."

"It's not about the money," Goldberg said. "I just want the clarinet."

"I knew it! You cheated!" Ivan said, sweeping the money up. "You get nothing!"

"I'll settle for the clarinet."

"Nothing!" He poked Goldberg in the chest with a bony finger.

"Just the clarinet. You keep the money … "

"I'll keep the money, all right. *And* the clarinet." This time he shoved Goldberg.

Patience, Goldberg told himself, and when Ivan closed his right hand into a fist and sent a looping roundhouse at the rabbi's head, a lightning quick jab to Ivan's forehead sent his eyes rolling. When he regained focus, he sprang toward Goldberg, swinging wildly. Dollar bills and coins scattered.

A forearm blocked one punch. Goldberg sidestepped another. Ivan kept swinging and Goldberg kept dodging until Ivan was winded. Then Ivan lowered his right for one more mighty punch. It was the opening Goldberg sought. The rabbi's left hook connected with a sickening smack. That Ivan remained conscious surprised Goldberg. And disappointed him, for a moment. But the man was clearly done.

"Just the clarinet," Goldberg said.

Ivan, with his eyes already swelling shut from the impact, mumbled, "Take it."

"And the old man gets his corner back."

Ivan spat blood and nodded. He rose to his knees and then finally to his feet, waving gently like wheat in the wind. Even as he wobbled, he looked calm—as if the anger had been knocked from him. Yet there was a clarity in his eyes as he studied the rabbi. A smile creased his pockmarked face and he looked into the distance as if he saw someone he knew and loved. He stepped in that direction ...

It's hard to know for sure if it was the punch that caused him to step out in front of that truck. Or maybe it was suicide.

Goldberg thought it was poetic the way the sun seemed to shove the clouds aside as the body twitched its last. He did not rush out after Ivan. Even at a distance, Goldberg could see that nothing could be done. He picked up only the money he had come with and then serenely hugged Artie Shaw's old clarinet to his chest, watching as winos and high-heeled hookers chased after fluttering greenbacks in the gutter. Someone took Ivan's fake Rolex off his wrist.

The cops cleared the trembling trucker of any wrongdoing and sent him on his way with his load of California oranges. It was just coincidence a few years later when the very same truck driver mowed down a cowboy named

Snake Western outside a Charming, Nevada, brothel. The Nevada highway patrol concluded that, too, was an unfortunate accident. But Peterbilt lost his job anyway. Two dead pedestrians were two too many.

In the end, Peterbilt was fired for being unlucky.

chapter Thirty-Two

In the dingy shops, Christmas lights twinkled. Even the kosher butcher strung some lights in the windows among the corpses of chickens. Hookers dressed like elves, and the drug dealer wore a Santa suit.

Hooter and Luxom DeShane sat on milk crates and drank it all in. Luxom took longer breaks these days. Ivan had taken something out of him that he never got back. Even as he sat in silence, clutching his clarinet, someone dropped a dollar into the box that read It's Been a Hard Day's Night.

Hooter wondered about the dollar. Was it for songs past or songs to come? The street seemed more optimistic since Ivan's demise.

"Whatcha doin' here, boy? You got the fancy job, the fancy woman, whatcha doin' here?" Luxom prodded.

"I missed the music," Hooter said, but the truth was, he missed Luxom.

"You don't need to check up on me."

"Hey, is there any law against a guy wanting to hear a little clarinet?"

The pail drummer was back, pounding away across the street. Sometimes Luxom tried to play along, but the kid always lost the beat or took off on some tangent. *Drummers.*

"Luxom, I've been wondering … "

"'Bout what?"

"The clarinet. Why is it so … "

"Important?"

"Yeah."

Luxom studied the instrument. "Artie Shaw gave it to me the day he fired me. I didn't know how to take that for the longest time. Artie broke up the band from time to time, but he never got rid of me. I was always on time, on key, and a damn good saxophone player too. I never played clarinet in the band back then. If anyone was going to play clarinet, it was Artie Shaw. He was the King of Swing! I used to honk away on the clarinet in the hotel rooms, and that's where Artie heard me one morning. The door was open a crack, I guess, and he just walked in and listened. Geez, can you imagine? I stopped playing, of course. But he waved me on, so I played. He listened a good twenty minutes, and then he left without a word. When he returned, he had his clarinet in his hand. He gave it to me, and then he fired me. I tried to get an explanation, but that's the way Artie was.

"So for the first time in almost a year, I went back home. But the house was empty. My wife and son, gone. She had taken up with another man, an importer. They moved to Chicago. That's what I heard. I always promised I'd be back. I told Eldrick—my son—that every time I left.

"I don't blame her for leaving. She was a sweet gal, and what good is a man that ain't there? I was young and greedy and selfish. I just cared more about me and my music than anyone else. It cost me. I just couldn't find the balance. What good is a life if you can't share it with someone?" The old man stared out at the street, not really seeing anything but the regrets replaying in his mind.

"I had it, Hooter! I had it," he said. "And I just gave it away.

"I gathered up a few boys and started playing, but that was in 1954, and the big band era had about run its course. We bounced around jazz clubs, but I just got tired of the road. So tired. … One day I just stopped. This just happened to be the place.

"I didn't realize it at the time, but Artie Shaw never played again. I mean, how could you know he had stopped for good? But time passed, decades, and he never played again. Can you imagine what it was like to realize such a thing? I wondered if I had made him quit. Sometimes I think—and these are immodest moments—that Artie realized I was wasted on the saxophone."

"Were you?" Hooter asked.

"I didn't think so. I was playing with Artie Shaw! I would have played maracas. I look back on it now and I think when Artie gave me that clarinet, he was passing the torch. There I was. Artie Shaw had chosen me as a successor, but I didn't have the heart for the road anymore. The road had taken everything from me. I didn't want any part of it. But I had to play. It would have been wrong not to play. I just started playing on this corner one day, and people started tossing money. So I never left. I wondered sometimes if Artie would have been embarrassed by what I was doing."

Another passerby tossed some quarters into the box.

"I suppose I'd better earn my keep," Luxom said as he rose. He looked at the feeble Christmas lights blinking out hopeful messages in Morse code in such a hopeless place. "Sometimes I wonder … "

"What?"

"I wonder if someday Eldrick might happen to walk by and hear me. He wouldn't know me. I wouldn't know him, but that would be enough for me. That my son would hear the music, maybe, and somewhere deep inside find a way to forgive me … "

He began to play.

Hooter recognized the tune but could not place it at first. It was from John Lennon's last recordings: "Beautiful Boy."

chapter Thirty-Three

How Hooter managed to run Wilma's gauntlet as many times as he did is hard to say. Miracles. Persistence. Dumb luck. She eyed him as he passed the receptionist's desk in his disguise. Each day Hooter felt he was one day closer to being revealed as a fraud.

An overflowing patient load weighed him down too. Patients recommended him to friends. Sure, Dr. Hooter Pridley had unusual methods, but they were effective. Word got around. He was a hit, but he could not enjoy it. He felt like a juggler. The longer he juggled, the closer he was to disaster. Inevitably something would fall. In no time at all Hooter Pridley became a prickly man.

After several terse sessions with Marshall E. Musters, a director who could no longer live on the reputation of his early classics—*The Willow Bends in the Whispering Wind* and *Mystic Hermit*—and was being shunned by producers, Hooter lost his temper.

"Why do you wanna blame everyone else for your problems? My grandpa always said we create most of our own problems. The problem is, you're an asshole," Hooter said.

Holy shit! No one had talked to the great man like that since, well, *ever*. Actors feared him, studio executives feared him, and somewhere along the way, he had begun to equate their fear with respect, when in reality it was disdain.

Musters glared for a long time. Then he chuckled. "That's your diagnosis? I'm an asshole? I could have told you that!"

"Yeah, well, you still have to pay me," Hooter said sullenly.

"So what would you have me do? No one will give me a job.'

"Anyone can get a job. There's always a job."

"Evidently. They give great scripts to pond scum, and they offer me dog meat."

"My grandpa always said that with a little elbow grease, even a dull knife cuts carrots. And a sharp knife ain't no good in the drawer."

• • •

What do you know—Musters swallowed his pride and took a dog meat script and turned it into filet mignon. Under budget, even. *Dangerous Heaven* stunned the critics. Burt Reynolds was, dare I say, brilliant. Fans filled the theaters. The old master was back, and he was almost *nice*, the insiders said. The man who disdained the press gave interviews, and he was borderline charming.

Hooter added his own thoughts about Marshall E. Musters in his file of Grandpa's sayings. "Being in a dark hole is bad enough," Hooter mused, "but you can't start digging out until you see the light."

Hooter's job, as he imagined it, was to simply hand his patients a shovel and tell them to start digging, just like the dowser Jack Lipensky had done to Hooter the day the Mormons struck oil in Utah.

The list of Hooter's success stories lengthened.

Zippy Nightshade was recording again, and word was he

was even more vile and disgusting than before. The album *Gory Details of a Demented Mind* was entrenched atop the charts. Teenagers loved him, and so did parents, though neither constituency willingly disclosed the information to the other. Unintentional as it was, Zippy Nightshade was bringing families together. MTV did a *Zippy Unplugged* special. Ed Bradley from *60 Minutes* interviewed him. They compared earrings. Zippy got a slew of Grammy nominations. He had never even been nominated before, and he was nervous about it—something he would never confess to anyone but Hooter.

"What if I don't win?"

"Well, you *already* didn't win. Lots of times."

"Yeah."

"But you always sold a pile of records. Why was that?" Hooter asked.

"'Cause we was too fuckin' edgy for polite society. Rebels."

"So if you don't win, you're still too edgy."

"Yeahhh," Zippy said slowly and smiled. Then a thought came to him that unnerved him. "What if I *do* win?"

"It means you sell a shitload of records."

"Yeahhh," he said, and his smile broadened. He pulled two tickets from his pocket. "I'd like you to be there," he said.

"That's nice, but I don't think so. I don't like crowds."

"I'll send my blood red limo. It would mean a lot to me."

"The blood red limo?" *The famous blood red limo!*

Trixie Foxalot was ecstatic about the invitation too. She immediately called her favorite designer to arrange a fitting.

By then Hooter rarely spent much time in his apartment. Although the arrangement had never been formalized, he had effectively moved into Trixie's modest mansion. It felt like paradise when he watched Trixie Foxalot sunbathing nude by the pool. Some days he just watched her for hours. Sometimes, for a change of pace, he would walk to the driveway and admire his 1970 orange Barracuda. Both were magnificent machines. Some days it all seemed so idyllic. Like a really happy soap opera.

"I love you, Hooter," Trixie would coo as she gazed adoringly at him.

"I love you, too," he would answer. He felt obligated to say it, though Hooter had never managed to spit out the words to Gladys Neidermeyer even once in six years. The one time he had tried, he got the name wrong. Trixie said it all the time, but she said it in the manner with which people answer the phone.

They were two people in love with the idea of being in love.

"Now, will you run out and get me a pack of cigarettes, honey?" Trixie would ask after the *I love yous*. How does one say no after that?

Hooter sighed. "I'll just get a carton this time," he said.

"No, don't do that. I'm trying to quit." Smokers have a logic all their own.

• • •

Things get on a person's nerves after a while. Every relationship is filled with little peeves and irritations like that. They build, they grow, and then there is the avalanche.

"I'm not entirely sure men and women should live together," Grandpa Pridley confided to Hooter one day at the fish shack. It was one of his more revolutionary thoughts, and he never said it in front of Grandma.

Trixie's irritating habits hadn't approached avalanche proportions for Hooter. What bothered him, though, was that he could never seem to engage Trixie in a meaningful discussion about an end to war—she seemed indifferent to the whole topic. And that had been the one factor above all that had led him to her. She was more than breasts and hair. She had an intellect and she wanted world peace. That's what was advertised in her own handwriting in *Plaything* magazine. He grew impatient waiting for Trixie's depth to emerge.

But his impatience was nothing compared to hers. Sometimes he thought she was short with her hairstylist. And rude to her manicurist. And the gardener. She even got testy when Hooter would not let her drive his "precious Barracuda." Trixie thought that meant he didn't love her. But no one else had ever driven that car. No one. It was sacred.

Trixie still snored and made sounds like Zippy Nightshade when they made love, and that troubled Hooter immensely. He was almost grateful when erectile dysfunction set in. Trixie seemed to handle his flaccidity with grace. She still proudly clung to his arm when they went out. It did not occur to Hooter that *he* was the trophy.

"She's fantastic," Horowitz said when he met her.

That's only because you didn't hear her speak, Hooter thought.

Trixie smiled coyly and nodded during introductions. It seemed aloof and icy, but most of all mysterious. Men just love that sort of thing.

Horowitz's divorce was going badly. He was grateful the business was setting new records, otherwise the lawyers would have bankrupted him. He was lonely. He missed his wife but couldn't really blame her for her vengeful, spiteful legal attacks.

He tried calling Van Horn's wife for a fling, but she turned him down. She and Van Horn were considering a reconciliation, she said. "My husband says you only seduced me to hurt him. Is that right, Benjamin?"

Horowitz denied it, *but damn*, he thought as he retracted his hand from the cookie jar, *Van Horn is good!*

Some evenings, after a few drinks, he drove past the prostitutes, but never worked up the courage to stop. One night, as he cruised Sunset Boulevard and was distracted by the merchandise in fishnet stockings, he was forced to make an abrupt stop when the light changed. The tires squealed and the front wheels skidded into the crosswalk. He turned his head sheepishly to see how many people had seen the embarrassing stop.

His eyes came to rest on a clarinet player on the corner. Their eyes met, and both widened. The great Professor Helmut Schlossenpfennig, Master of the Mind, was playing a clarinet for quarters on Sunset Boulevard.

chapter Thirty-Four

"So," said Horowitz as he sat on the edge of Hooter's desk the next morning, like a cat ready to pounce, "tell me about Mount Evans University … "

"Uhh, well … that's where I studied Freud and Jung."

"And as I recall from the resume, you were at the top of your class?"

"Way high above everyone else." Hooter settled into his chair, reclining so he could appear to be more relaxed than he was.

Horowitz sadly shook his head and waved his hand as if he could brush away the lies. "Before you dig any deeper, I want to tell you that I saw Helmut Schlossenpfennig last night."

Hooter's chair tipped over backward, slamming his head against the wall. He felt like fainting. To his dismay he remained conscious.

"He was playing the clarinet," Horowitz continued, not missing a beat. "He was quite good, actually—but then, *he is a genius*."

"I'm sorry," Hooter said, scrambling to his feet, "I … I … "

"Who are you, really?"

"Oh, I'm really Hooter Pridley." He dusted off his pants.

"I mean, what is your real profession?"

"Parts man. But I can do lots of things … "

"Evidently."

Horowitz was sincerely hurt by the fraud. He really was. He had also already calculated that Hooter's fall would bring about his own financial ruin. It would be a huge scandal. He would lose everything. He would never be licensed again. He had cut corners. He had been swept away by desperation, ego, and a really good clarinet player on Sunset Boulevard. No background checks. The word of Helmut Schlossenpfennig had been enough. He had been such a fool.

Hooter did some calculating of his own. He would lose everything he had come here for. He would lose Trixie Foxalot. He would go back home humbled.

He would probably end up ice fishing.

"You have such a gift," Horowitz said. "If you had botched your cases, this wouldn't be such a tragedy."

"Nope, I never did no botching."

"But you've actually made people's lives *better*. And what's more, they keep coming back because they like you!"

Hooter's chest puffed. He began to get a little emotional thinking about all the good he had done. He had gotten Satan's Ghoul back on track, hadn't he?

"It's a pity it has to end," Horowitz said.

"A pity," Hooter said.

"But perhaps we shouldn't be too hasty."

"Haste makes waste."

"We should think this through."

"Thinking is good," Hooter said, though it was generally an abstract theory to him.

"Sometimes I think for months before I make a decision."

"Months," Hooter repeated hopefully. "Nothing wrong with that."

"I'll give this some thought," Horowitz said. "But I warn you, this will take a great deal of thinking. I might not come to a solution for years, even."

"I understand," Hooter said. "You want to make sure you do the right thing."

They shook hands.

"Well, our problems are solved for the moment," Horowitz said.

"There's still a problem," Hooter said. "I think Wilma is on to me."

• • •

Wilma the receptionist was fired that day. She was furious, in spite of a ninety-day severance package. But it was a short-lived unemployment—Van Horn took her on at a better salary. His clientele was growing. Not many stars, but when you get right down to it, a nutcase is a nutcase.

chapter Thirty-Five

It was a triumph. On Valentine's Day Zippy Nightshade won two Grammys: Album of the Year, and Song of the Year for the ballad "Embalm Me, Baby (And I'm Yours Forever)."

The crowd gave him a standing ovation both times he won. Trixie Foxalot jumped to her feet from the front row, and her breasts nearly fell out of her low-cut dress. The director couldn't resist. He kept cutting to her as they panned the audience. Her beauty was magnetic. She clutched Hooter's tuxedoed arm excitedly as Zippy thanked God for being so supportive of his evil ways. Zippy thanked his manager, his newest wife, his agent, Balderdash Records, and "last but not least, the man most responsible for me being here, the best *effing* shrink in the *effing* world, Dr. *effing* Hooter Pridley!"

The camera zoomed in on Hooter and Trixie.

At home, watching with a fistful of popcorn, Wilma, the fired receptionist, nearly choked. Her mouth was full, so she could only elbow her husband.

"I know," her husband said, "will you get a load of those knockers!"

"No," she said, after she swallowed. She walked closer to the television, hoping the camera would flash back to Hooter, which it did. "I know him," Wilma said.

• • •

At Zippy's raucous post-Grammy party, the A-list was there. Gene Simmons hovered over Trixie, waggling his tongue, but Hooter couldn't do much about it. He was inundated by celebrities trying to meet the man who had resurrected Zippy Nightshade. Some tried to make appointments. Others tried to get dreams interpreted. One extremely drunk actress got hysterical about repressed-memory issues. Pretty much everyone there claimed to have been sexually molested as a child.

Trixie worked her way though the crowd to get to Zippy. After all, he was the star of the evening. From across the room, where he was trapped by a yammering record producer with a Glock in his waistband, Hooter could see Zippy's face grow from puzzlement to anger as he talked to Trixie. What could she possibly be saying to upset him? She *was* a bit tipsy. Abruptly spinning on his heel, Zippy stalked toward Hooter.

"What's with your woman?"

"Why?"

"She's mocking me."

"How? What do you mean?"

"She's doing impersonations of me. Her voice is dead-on. Sure, maybe it was a little funny at first, but she just don't know when to quit!"

"You don't get it, Zippy. That's her voice. Her real voice."

Zippy gave Hooter a look of combined incredulity and pity. "Jesus!" he said. "Nice tits, though."

"Thanks. I, uh … " A disturbance distracted him. There was a scuffle at the door, and Zippy rushed off to see what was happening just as an inebriated Trixie wobbled over with Gene Simmons hot on the trail.

"Wash going on?" Trixie asked.

Simmons stopped dead in his tracks when he heard that awful voice. It reminded him of Dick Butkus.

Hooter stood on his toes to see the scuffle. "It's David Lee Roth. I think he was trying to sneak in again … Look, it's late, what do you say we call it a night? I'm bushed."

"Are you kidding! Itch only two A.M.," Trixie slurred. "This could go on for hours. I didn't even get to talk to Gene Simmons yet. Baby, pleeease." Trixie wobbled as if the wind were blowing inside the room.

"We're going," Hooter snapped as he pulled Trixie, teetering on spike heels, to the car. She was furious. She refused to speak to him on the ride home, which was fine with Hooter. She remained silent as they entered her estate.

Later Hooter could hear her banging around in the kitchen cabinets. Then she appeared at his side looking mussed but trying to be sexy.

"Baby," she purred—the way a water buffalo purrs.

"Yeah?" he sighed.

"Be a dear and run out and get some cigarettes for me, will you?"

"It's almost three A.M."

"I know, baby," she said, stroking his inner thigh, to no effect. "I would get them myself, but the Mercedes is in the shop. *Remember?*"

Hooter yawned and stretched out on the bed, his eyes closed. "In the morning. I'll get them in the morning … " And he was asleep.

Trixie was vexed. First they had to leave the party early and now her amazing body wasn't enough to make a man leap up and drive a few blocks to get her cigarettes. And she really needed a cigarette! *Gene Simmons* would have gotten her a cigarette. *He* knew how to treat a lady!

She hardly hesitated when she saw Hooter's car keys hanging by the refrigerator. She would show him.

It was her intention to burn rubber all the way down

to the street, but the car was too much for her. She hammered the accelerator and the car lurched forward and immediately began fishtailing out of control at forty miles per hour. She was flung toward the passenger door with her foot still pressed against the accelerator.

The engine roared like a jet at takeoff, the tires squealed, and then ...

Hooter bolted upright in bed. *What the hell was that?* He sprinted out the door in just his underwear. The dew chilled his bare feet as he ran.

It was a terrible sight. In the collision between the vintage 1970 Barracuda and the concrete pillar at the end of the drive, the pillar was the clear victor. The hood was wrinkled backward and fluttered in the air like a broken wing. Smoke wafted from the engine, fluids drained onto the grass, and Trixie Foxalot was slumped in the front seat. Hooter rushed to rescue her.

"So sorry," she said drunkenly as he opened the door, which hung for a moment on one hinge before falling off completely.

She had a cut at her hairline, but it wouldn't require stitches, Hooter decided. She had not been wearing a seat belt, but Hooter surmised that Trixie Foxalot's prodigious breasts had saved her from grievous injury. He carried her into the bedroom and gently cleaned her face with a warm, wet towel. She seemed to be fine. *He* was the one in shock. She had killed the Barracuda. What's more, she didn't seem to feel any remorse about it.

As Hooter seethed, Trixie disrobed tipsily in the bathroom and strutted out naked. "I'll make it up to you, baby," she said.

Hooter looked up. What he saw shocked him. And he began screaming.

"What? *What?*" Trixie asked.

Hooter pointed at her torso, and she frantically ran her hands over her body to discover the injury. She expected to find inner organs protruding. When she reached her left breast, she began screaming too. Her right breast stood majestic and proud. Her left breast had been reduced to a flat, floppy flap of tan skin. There was no wound, no blood. Her breast had deflated upon impact like a cheap balloon.

Until that moment, Hooter Pridley was the only man in the free world who did not suspect that Trixie Foxalot's breasts held enough saline to fill reservoirs. It was the final betrayal. There she stood with her flat left breast, her flat ass, and her gravel truck voice. She had killed the Barracuda. And that whole thing about world peace—it was a sham too.

Hooter realized he had been hating her for quite some time. As he thought about it, he realized he hated himself, too, for being so stupid. He slowly got dressed.

"Please, don't go, Hooter."

He reached for his jacket and put the tie in his pocket.

"But if you're going out, it's Marlboro Light 100s."

"I won't be back." In his tuxedo, he felt like James Bond.

"But I need you," she said. "I love you."

It almost sounded like she meant it, but Hooter Pridley walked out on his dream girl without another word. He couldn't imagine things getting any worse. His car—that wonderful car—was dead. Trixie Foxalot's tit had gone flat as the calendar he had first seen it on. It had been as much of an illusion as their relationship. If she had really loved him, she wouldn't have driven the car. Gladys Neidermeyer never drove the car. She drove a Ford Taurus.

As he walked past the steaming shambles of the Barracuda, Hooter thought, *Life cannot possibly get any worse.*

Funny thing about life. Sometimes life takes assertions like that as a challenge.

chapter Thirty-Six

Hooter Pridley did not sleep that night. He walked the streets for hours in a tuxedo, feeling like James Bond—but without the really cool car. He smoked a pack of cigarettes and spent half an hour being consoled—in conversation only—by a hooker named Lottie Love. He had lost his car *and* his girl on Valentine's Day.

When Hooter didn't appear at the office the next morning, Horowitz began to worry.

"Still no Dr. Pridley? Wha—, wha—?"

Horowitz opened the door wider to better survey the disaster in Hooter's waiting room. Molly McDonald had almost finished disassembling the desk. She looked up and smiled. Horowitz couldn't help but smile back.

"One of the drawers got stuck," she explained. "I took it apart to see how it worked. It's quite clever. All the rollers and slides … But once I started taking all the screws out, I had to keep going … "

"I see," said Horowitz. In her own daft way, she was really quite remarkable. There was a certain earnestness about her that he had come to appreciate. She didn't try to conceal her demons, and that was refreshing.

"He'll be a little late," Molly said.

"Who?"

"Dr. Pridley."

"Oh, yeah."

"He said he had car trouble ... "

Horowitz was working up the nerve to ask her on a date when he saw her eyes shift and focus past him. She looked alarmed. Horowitz turned and came eye to eye with Van Horn. Wilma, the fired receptionist, stood smugly behind him, arms defiantly folded.

"We have business to discuss," Van Horn said.

"We have *nothing* to discuss," Horowitz said. "What's this all about?"

"I have some paperwork for you. You're going to sign the business over to me."

Horowitz stared. "You have to know I won't do that!" he sputtered. "It's laughable."

"What I do know is that your cash cow is a janitor. *That's* what's laughable. It seems Wilma remembered Pridley as an applicant for the janitorial position."

Wilma nodded.

"But ... but ... the business ... I can't just *give* you the business," Horowitz said. He was pale. Even for a normally pale man, he was pale. He could have passed for Edgar Winter.

"You're not really giving me the business," Van Horn said. "Technically, it's a purchase. One dollar. But it won't be worth even that if you don't sign. When word gets out about your little charade, the business will be ruined. You'll lose your license. You'll be finished."

"And if I sign?"

"Mum's the word. I won't say a word about your little escapade. Neither will Wilma. You get to start over. Just like I did. It's a generous offer, all things considered."

Horowitz was stunned into silence. Finally he managed a sentence. "When?"

"Now," said Van Horn. "My movers are waiting outside with my things."

"Th—, th—, that's rather presumptuous, isn't it?" Horowitz asked.

"Clean out your desk," Van Horn said. "And I trust you'll see to it that the staff remains intact—through the transition, at least."

"But ... but ... "

"What?" Van Horn snarled.

"I ... I want *her*," Horowitz said.

Molly McDonald was surprised to see him pointing at her, and then pleased.

"She stays," Van Horn said, twisting the knife.

"Hold it!" Molly said, stepping between them. "I'm not a piece of meat!"

"I'll triple your salary and double your vacation benefits!" Van Horn said.

Wilma scowled.

"You too!" Van Horn amended.

Molly shrugged at Horowitz. "I'm meat."

"But ... but ... ," Horowitz said.

"The deal's off, unless she stays through the transition," Van Horn said.

With a trembling hand, Benjamin Horowitz signed away a lifetime's worth of labor for one dollar.

A minute later he walked woodenly toward the parking lot, where he met Hooter walking in.

"You're fired," Horowitz told him. "Let's have a drink, and I'll tell you about it."

• • •

Van Horn beamed as Wilma directed the movers. Vengeance. It was delicious. Workmen began cracking open crates and hanging paintings.

"Look," Van Horn bragged to Molly. "Jackson Pollocks. Nineteen of them. I bought a collection last month. Almost stole it, really. They've already increased in value fifteen percent!"

"Nice ... ," Molly said. Her fingers began to twitch.

chapter Thirty-Seven

Hooter called his favorite patients from the bar to say good-bye. The loofah sponge heiress had made remarkable progress. She was still hearing voices, but now it was Vin Scully, and the Dodgers were up three to two in the sixth. Desmond Carson was virtually cured. Of course, he claimed to have a fear of kidney beans, which would have meant inventing a whole new phobia. But Hooter told Desmond that lots of people didn't like one food or another.

"It's perfectly normal," he said.

"I'm still scared," Desmond replied

"Just don't stab anyone," Hooter said, and Desmond never did.

Hooter recommended Horowitz as a replacement to all of his patients.

"But ... but I can't possibly do what you do," Horowitz said.

"I wrote it all down—everything my grandpa ever told me and a few things I came up with on my own," Hooter said. "Molly will get you the file. It's yours. The rest is just acting interested and nodding once in a while."

"I know that! Christ, I went to Harvard, you know."

• • •

He was deep into a recording session when he got the call, but Zippy Nightshade insisted on seeing Hooter one more time in person. Horowitz and Hooter were on their fifth vodkas when he arrived. Zippy settled for seltzer water.

Satan's Ghoul drummed his fingers on the table. Hooter recognized it as the beat from "Slice Me, Dice Me, Ice Me." Zippy was nervous. Facing life without Hooter Pridley to back him up was like the first day without training wheels.

"But what if I fucking fall apart again?" he asked.

"You fucking won't," Hooter said.

"How do you fucking know?" Zippy asked.

"Because I'm a fucking doctor," Hooter said.

That was good enough for Zippy. Fucking case closed. He slugged his seltzer and checked his watch. "I suppose I should get back. We're working on a duets album. Alice Cooper and Kiss are coming in next week. I'm recording with Iggy Pop right now."

"Bet it will be great," Hooter said.

"It'll be shit," Zippy grinned. "And we'll probably sell millions—if I can talk Iggy out of using strings and a clarinet. A sax, maybe, but, Christ, a clarinet?"

"I know a sax player," Hooter said.

"It ain't Kenny G, is it?"

• • •

"It's a good thing you did for him," Horowitz said as Zippy walked out to a smattering of applause from the bar crowd. He roared off in the blood red limo with the Lon Chaney hood ornament.

"Yeah, but I'm sorry about the mess I made of your life," Hooter said.

"I caused the mess," Horowitz said. "You just helped me smear it around a bit. The business would have gone down without Van Horn anyway. What was the worst thing that happened in the interim? You helped a few people. No one got hurt."

"Wilma got fired," Hooter said.

"That was bad," Horowitz said.

"Pretty bad."

"But otherwise," Horowitz said, raising his glass, "a pretty good run."

Thirty-Eight

With the good-byes coming to a close, the tug of home grew stronger. Hooter wanted to be back in Sterling, Colorado, so badly, he ached. Even if there are no mountains there. It was hard to imagine driving back in anything but the Barracuda, but life rolls on forever, even if classic Plymouths don't.

Hooter mourned the death of the Barracuda for some time—a reasonable grieving period for a car, anyway. But within days he found a promising ad in the *Los Angeles Times* that led him to a body shop in Encino and a masterfully chopped 1955 Ford Fairlane with a jazzed-up 351 wedged under the hood on a late model frame and suspension.

It was quicker off the line than the Barracuda had been, but it didn't have the top end. The car was jet black with three-inch headers that violated noise regulations in the next county. It wasn't the same as building your own monster, but still, it was some car.

He could have bought it cheaper, but the negotiation got excruciating. The man wanted twenty-six thousand dollars. Hooter offered twenty-three. The man countered with "twenty f-f-f- ... " He stuttered, and now it made sense to Hooter why the man referred to the 1955 Ford Fairlane as simply "the car." At first it bothered Hooter that such a sublime machine should be lumped into a category. Now

Hooter felt helpless as the *F*s went sputtering along. He found himself negotiating for both of them.

"How about twenty-five fifty?"

The man seemed offended. "Twenty f-f-f- ... "

It was clear the seller would not settle for any amount that had fives in it.

"Twenty-six it is," Hooter said. "Who should I make the check to?"

"F-f-f- ... Frank Ph-ph-ph-ilips."

As he drove away, Hooter found himself smiling, really smiling, for the first time in days. It came to him that even when times were good with Trixie and in the early heady days as a psychologist, his greatest joy each day had come when he was alone, driving on the LA freeways. He found himself falling in love again—with a chopped 1955 Ford with three-inch headers.

Luxom DeShane stopped playing when Hooter rumbled up to the curb.

"Nice," he said. "Brings back memories. Used to have one myself. Stock, of course, but a real dandy. But what happened to the Barracuda?"

Hooter explained about Trixie and the car and how he had lost his job.

"That's tough," Luxom said.

"Yeah," Hooter said. "But everything worked out like I wanted. For a while."

"Were you happy before it all fell apart?"

"Not really. I got everything I thought I wanted ... "

Luxom smiled knowingly. "So now what?"

"I'm gonna go home. See if anyone's waiting for me."

"I hope there is. So where is home, exactly?"

"Sterling, Colorado."

"Sounds nice. I'll bet the mountains are beautiful," Luxom said.

"They are," Hooter sighed. Why fight it? "You could ride along, if you're not doing anything."

"Funny thing," Luxom said. "Some producer gave me his card and told me to be at Balderdash Records tomorrow morning. They need a sax player."

"Imagine that," Hooter said.

"Some guy named Itchy Pot wants me."

"Iggy Pop, and he's a legend."

"Yeah, well, so am I. One thing, though—I wonder how he knew I play sax."

"The Lord works in mysterious ways."

"Don't he, though." Luxom ran his fingers along the chrome fins of the car. "Mine was aqua and white. We took it on a picnic the day I bought it—me and Janie and Eldrick. They couldn't get over how beautiful it was. Even when we were eating, they stared at it. And me, I remember staring at them, because *they* were so beautiful. I wonder how I ever lost sight of that ... " He peered in the window. "Can I drive it?"

"Sure," said Hooter. "Let's go."

Luxom DeShane shook off forty years behind the wheel. The car took him back to a time before he made the selfish mistakes that set his path askew. They cruised Sunset Boulevard and Colorado Boulevard and every other boulevard worth cruising. Hooter realized later that in his last hours with Luxom DeShane, they hardly spoke at all. They smiled wistful smiles that had to serve as farewells and other things such men leave unsaid. Ships pass in the night, and so do 1955 Fords.

They drove to the synagogue to say good-bye to Rabbi Goldberg, but he was in Jerusalem.

chapter **Thirty-Nine**

Officially, the distance between Los Angeles and Sterling, Colorado, is 1,140 miles, but it feels farther than that. The distance traveled is not always measured in miles or inches or centimeters or meters. Sometimes it is measured in bumps and bruises, heartache and disappointment.

Dear Hooter, our traveler wrote in his journal, *I'm going home. I'm sad. But it's not the going home that makes me sad. I think it's because I don't love Trixie Foxalot anymore. I never hated anyone before. It would have been better if I just loved her calendar and never met her. Grandpa always said, "Be careful what you wish for." But that doesn't stop me from wishing I was back with Gladys Neidermeyer …*

Hooter's grandfather also advised witnessing beautiful things whenever possible. Sometimes he would pull his old pickup to an approach just to watch a particularly striking sunset. That wasn't the smartest thing to do, because the headlights didn't work in that old truck. But then they would drive in the dark and admire the moon. You could call it a quirk, but deep inside, Hooter's grandfather understood something that most men never do. While it is all fine and good to pursue dreams and all the hope that comes with that, one must be careful not to ignore the good dreams in the present.

Once he detoured the family vacation to Devil's Tower in Wyoming over everyone's objections. *Why would anyone want to look at a stupid rock?* But they all treasured that afternoon and the memory of that pillar jutting up out of nowhere.

That day produced the best Pridley family pictures ever snapped. They were displayed on mantels and walls over any number of states. The family was gathered at the base of that big rock, grinning as if they'd never had a care. And Grandpa looked pleased to be standing there with his children and grandchildren. He looked so proud, you might have thought he was the one who put that big beautiful rock there. Hooter was only eight in the picture, and he didn't remember many details of the day, just the immensity of the rock and an unfettered joy. Looking at that picture and remembering that day just made him feel good.

It was with his grandfather's advice in mind that Hooter detoured to the Grand Canyon. He had heard it was something one should see before dying. Not that he felt like dying, but his heart was broken, and that pretty much feels like the same thing.

Yes, there was joy in the powerful 1955 Ford Fairlane lovingly built by a man who could not say its name. Hooter marveled at the balance and stability of the suspension. This, unlike a thousand Jackson Pollocks, was art. The car kept Hooter from weeping. The endless strip of blacktop gave him ample time to consider the road he had traveled.

He drove without a map, looping through small towns for gas at rickety stations run by toothless old ladies when a map might have told him about the shiny, impersonal superstation just a few miles ahead, with urinals that read your mind and know when to flush.

Grandpa Pridley didn't believe in maps. "The good Lord is the only one who really knows what lies ahead," he said. "And I don't need a road map to tell me where I've been." To Hooter, that always sounded like the lyrics to a country song.

He considered the point Grandpa Pridley was trying to make about maps. Maps are for people who hold the illusion that they know where they are going. Driving without a map takes faith. This is not to disparage Rand McNally or plans and goals in general. But just because directions get put down on paper doesn't mean those folks know the best route for you.

• • •

Hooter stared out at the Grand Canyon for hours, oblivious to the comings and goings of the other travelers. It truly was grand. It lived up to its name. It would be a pity if some malcontent had discovered the place and called it Decent Canyon. Who would travel across the country to see that?

Take the name Trixie Foxalot, for instance. If someone told you there was a woman in Los Angeles named Bertha Butz, would you go? No. So you can see why her agent wanted her to change her name and inflate her breasts. It was false advertising, because inside Trixie Foxalot was still Bertha Butz, with a voice that could peel paint. She was shallow, mean, and flatulent.

Gladys Neidermeyer wasn't as spectacular on the outside, but there was nothing false about her. Hooter desperately missed her enthusiasm for life, and particularly her enthusiasm for *him*. It was the gleam in her eyes and the quick smile that made her beautiful. Now, as he sat staring out into a void of rocks and cliffs and canyon, he could see it all plainly.

Hooter did not notice the wind subside as the sun began to set behind him. He did not notice that he was alone until a beleaguered station wagon filled with peering faces limped up. The muffler was wired on, as was the front bumper. It was a wheezing, smoke-belching, pitiful contrast to Hooter's shiny 1955 Fairlane.

The doors creaked open in the cloud of exhaust left by the engine, and seven children, ages two to twelve, stepped out along with their beaming parents. All the children were clad in clean but faded apparel, hand-me-downs from one child to the next. The smallest child's clothing was the most faded, and he had the biggest grin. One of his older brothers sauntered over to where Hooter was sitting.

"Hiyah, mister," the child said to Hooter as the rest of them gathered to watch the sun set over Grand Canyon. "Ain't it about the most purdiest thing you ever seen?"

Hooter looked at the joyful family. "Yes," he said. "Yes, it is."

"Daddy said, 'Everyone otter to see the Grand Canyon once before they die,'" the little chap informed Hooter.

"Dougie," the father said, "are you bothering the man?"

"No bother at all," Hooter said.

At that moment, the wire on the front bumper surrendered, and one end clanked to the blacktop. The father shrugged and unwired the other end. He cheerfully stashed the bumper in the back of the station wagon. "Sorry," he said, as if he had to apologize for his poverty. "It's not much to look at, but you do what you can do, don't you?"

Hooter nodded, embarrassed at his self-pity. It seemed shallow and out of place.

The man continued talking. "I wasn't sure we would make it. The car overheated along the way. That slowed us down some. But look at how beautiful the canyon is in the sunset. That clogged radiator gave us this gift." He surveyed his brood. Their eyes were wide with wonder at the hugeness of it all.

Hooter and the man stared out across the red light and the lengthening shadows. The man's voice broke above the murmur of the children. "I had to scrape to come up with enough money to do this," he confided. He smiled broadly. "But here we are." He was silent for a moment before he continued. "My daddy always promised to take us to here. He scrimped and saved, but he always put it off because he never believed he had quite enough to pay for hotels and cafes. There were nine kids, if you can believe it."

Hooter smiled wistfully.

"And no, we weren't Catholic," the man said, anticipating the question that always followed. "My family just believed in kids."

Believed in kids. The phrase echoed in Hooter's mind. *Believed in kids. Like some folks believe in God,* he thought. What a wonderful thing to believe in.

"I was here twenty-five years ago," the man said. "Five days after my twin brother, Eddie, had a tractor roll over him. Folks thought my dad was crazy for taking a vacation right after the funeral, but I always knew why. He realized then that you can't count on tomorrow. Eddie never got to see the Grand Canyon. Daddy didn't want that happening to the rest of us, and, well, I didn't want that happening to my kids."

You can't count on tomorrow. It sounded like something Hooter's grandfather might say. Hooter never recalled him saying it, but Grandpa Pridley lived it. Until that moment, Hooter never understood so clearly why his grandfather stopped sometimes to watch the sun set and the geese fly.

"Sorry about your brother," Hooter said.

"Oh, it was years ago," the man said, as if that made it less of a loss, as if sorrows cease being sorrows in time. They fade, they burrow deep, but they never leave. That's the truth of it. The man turned so Hooter could not see the tears welling.

"Thanks," Hooter said as he walked to his car. He wanted to, *needed to*, drive a few more miles closer to home.

The man wondered for a moment why he had been thanked, but the thought passed as he gathered up his children with prodding and hugs. They dined on minced-ham sandwiches under the glow of a Coleman lantern in a roadside park. They slept that night in ragged sleeping bags, the children unaware that their father was building a memory for them under the stars.

chapter Forty

When Hooter Pridley finally arrived in Sterling, Colorado, a wave of something he could not define washed over him and settled like a warm blanket. It's that feeling you get when you go home. It feels like you belong.

He had been so intent on getting there. When he reached the city limits, he realized he hadn't considered what he would do when he arrived. He no longer had a home.

It was habit that made him turn the wheel into Kum and Go. Topping off the tank would give him something constructive to do while he considered his next move. Shirley Baranskey was behind the register. As he set a Pepsi and a Milky Way on the counter, Hooter noticed that Shirley did not have her usual sad, slightly bedraggled look. Every gesture, every movement behind the till was dramatic, until Hooter finally caught on: she was waving a large diamond engagement ring.

"Nice ring," Hooter said. It was obvious she wanted to talk about it.

"Peter Wangdoodle and I are getting married next Saturday."

"Peter?" When Hooter left town, Peter was *married*.

"The divorce is final Thursday. We get married Saturday. Peter will be a bachelor for one day. We were going to go to the justice of the peace to get married right after the papers were finalized, but we decided on a church wedding."

"That's nice," Hooter said flatly, still trying to absorb all of this.

"I'm not a home wrecker, if that's what you're thinking," Shirley said.

That wasn't what Hooter was thinking. Much of the time Hooter wasn't thinking anything at all.

"The marriage just seemed to fall apart after the death of the cat," she continued. "That happens sometimes. Something like that can drive a wedge between two people."

Yes, cats are a leading cause of divorce.

"That's too bad," Hooter said. "I mean about the cat and the divorce. It's *good* that you're getting married. ... So how is Peter?"

"Oh, he works too hard. He's said more than once what a good parts man you were. I think he'd like to have you back."

A job seemed like a good idea, so Hooter motored to Wangdoodle Auto & Truck Parts. Customers were stacked in two lines, three deep. Peter was alone behind the counter. He looked up, then looked away when Hooter tried to catch his eye. While he waited, Hooter picked up a few things. Points and plugs, oil and a filter. He waited until the last customer was gone before plopping the merchandise on the counter.

"Hooter," Peter said.

"Peter."

"Stayin' outta trouble?"

"It's hard to comb my hair with the halo," Hooter said.

"They're horns," Peter said, but he was smiling good-naturedly when he said it. He studied the points. "These are for a Ford. What happened to the Barracuda?"

"Got wrecked."

"Criminy." He seemed genuinely sympathetic.

Hooter wished he could be equally empathetic about something just to let Peter know there were no hard feelings. "Sorry about your cat," he said.

Peter tried to change the subject. "Yeah, that was a bad deal, but—"

"It's tough losing a cat," Hooter said.

"Yeah, but—"

"Hard to find a good cat," Hooter said, which probably explains why he had never owned one. "But when a cat's time comes, nothin' you can do. We all gotta go sometime. Hope he didn't suffer … "

"No, it was over pretty fast," Peter said.

"That's a blessing."

Peter agreed that it was a blessing, even as he tried to shake the image of the strangled cat from his conscience. "Uh, so what brings you back to town?"

"Kinda missed it."

"Stayin' long?"

"Maybe."

"Need something to do while you decide?"

"Yeah," Hooter said. "Why not?"

"Well, if you want to work here, you can. Until you decide what you want to do."

"Sure. Okay. Until I decide."

They never mentioned the fight. That's men for you. No need to rehash a bad incident. There's no reason to talk about your feelings. Guys just ignore things until they forget about them. Women could take a few lessons from men. Women are the scientists of relationships. They want to examine and *reexamine* a conflict between a man and a woman until the man surrenders and confesses that it was all his fault—even if it wasn't.

• • •

Hooter circled Gladys Neidermeyer's house until the gas gauge sank noticeably. In the old days, men used to pace while they solved problems. With the advent of the car, men began driving in circles to solve their problems. Henry

Ford invented circling. You might say he modernized the whole thinking game.

When he finally worked up the courage to walk to the front door, Hooter found that a repellent force prevented him from knocking. He raised his knuckles, but they were stopped short of the door each time. This went on for several minutes, until Hooter finally broke through. The knocking sounded unsettlingly loud, even though it was tentative. The sound made Hooter want to run.

Now, about the bravest thing a man can do is face a horde of howling, blood-lusting enemy warriors in the heat of battle. A close second is facing a woman scorned.

He had not remembered just how pure and fresh Gladys Neidermeyer's pretty face was until the door opened. Her eyes mellowed, and her lip quivered. Then her eyes narrowed. Hooter's jaw dropped. Eventually he would have said something, but she slammed the door in his face.

He knocked again and was met with silence. He kept knocking, and she kept not answering. Hooter Pridley was a broken man.

He leaned his forehead against the door until it supported him, and began speaking to the door. "Gladys, I know I did you wrong. But I want you to know that I never stopped thinking about you. I remembered how good you were to me and ... Oh, I am such an idiot ... " And then Hooter Pridley said something to the door that he had never said to Gladys. "I love you."

The door flew open, and Hooter fell forward and landed inside, on his face. He looked up.

Gladys stood above him watching his nose drip blood onto the wood floor. In recent meetings between Hooter and Gladys Neidermeyer, Hooter's nose had gotten the worst of it.

"Say that again," Gladys said.

"I ... I love you," Hooter said.

"Not that."

Hooter blinked. His eyes watered from the pain. "Uh, I am an idiot?"

"Bingo," said Gladys.

She held an ice bag to his nose, which was not as cold as the silence. There was awkward chitchat, but mostly silence.

Gladys broke one of those silences by saying, "I suppose you might as well bring in your things."

At bedtime, Hooter followed Gladys into the bedroom and began unbuttoning his shirt.

"Hold it, mister," she said. "What do you think you're doing?"

"Sleeping on the couch?" Hooter guessed.

"Bingo," she said.

It was a love seat, really, but Hooter didn't feel that well loved as he slept. His feet hung over one armrest and it made his knees hurt. He thrashed miserably and consoled himself with the thought that it was far better than Maggie's Shithole.

He was surprised when he woke to find Gladys's hand touching his. He was surprised because he hadn't imagined that he had slept at all. But there she was, looking angelic in an oversized white cotton T-shirt as he blinked to consciousness. Her eyes had lost their steely glint. They were softer now.

"It's time for bed," she said. It was two A.M. Hooter followed her into the bedroom on achy knees. Beggars in Calcutta could not have been more grateful and over-whelmed than Hooter was in that moment.

"I'm an idiot," he said when they were under the sheets together, because he knew she liked hearing that. "But I'm an idiot who loves you ... " And so it went, the greatest soliloquy—*the only soliloquy*—of Hooter's life. He poured out, so earnestly, what was in his heart that Gladys forgave him. She did not forget—*women never forget*, and they never lose sight of the fact that men are pigs—but Gladys resolved to let him back into her heart. He had never left, really. He was entrenched there. That's what made it so hard to know that he had spent so much time looking past her and through her, never really seeing her.

Hooter hadn't meant to hurt her with his wandering eye. But even as women run deep as a pristine blue ocean, men are shallow, muddy puddles with drowned worms at the bottom.

Hooter Pridley was man enough to admit that he was wrong. There are no mountains in Sterling, Colorado. But in Sterling, Colorado, some men stand tall enough.

The End

That's where I wanted the book to end, anyway. I like happy endings. But then the publisher had to go asking all sorts of questions, like what happened to this person and that person, et cetera.

"What's the big deal?" I said. "The important thing is, Hooter Pridley realized the error of his ways and went back to a woman who truly loved him."

"I think you're holding out on us," the publisher said.

"Am not," I said.

"Are too."

"Am not."

"Are too."

That went on for some time, but in the interest of brevity, I won't bore you with it all. Eventually the publisher leaned across the table and said, "According to my calculations, you will make ten thousand dollars for each subsequent chapter."

"What's *subsequent* mean?" I asked. (For the record, it means the ones to follow.) "And what if they're short chapters?"

"You still get ten thousand dollars," he said. "Even for short ones."

There is a point in every artist's life when he is faced with a decision. Should he continue his noble, artistic path or compromise his vision in the interest of commerce? Every artist wrestles with it. Are you going to do Jackson Pollocks or velvet Elvises? These are all very good questions not to be taken lightly.

As Jack Benny famously said to the bandit who demanded his money or his life, "I'm thinking! I'm thinking."

chapter **Forty-One**

A month later, almost to the day, Trixie Foxalot blew into town in a gleaming orange 1970 Barracuda.

For Hooter and Gladys Neidermeyer, it had been a magical time. Their love, their commitment to each other, was renewed. It was stronger than before because they had experienced life without each other and had been lucky enough to bring it all back together. This is rare. Once true love separates, time and circumstance and the heavens themselves do not often consent to the reunion. That is why a love reunited is the sweetest of all.

Hooter was true blue, and Gladys—do you even have to ask? Of course she was true blue. Sure, Hooter still stared at pretty girls. All men do—unless they're dead, and I should mention that staring at pretty girls *is* a leading cause of death. Like marijuana, it leads to other things.

Personally, some folks I know—*and I'm not naming names*—think that if Hooter hadn't smoked pot on the first day of his journey to Hollywood, none of the tragic stuff that followed would have been so tragic. For instance, maybe Trixie Foxalot's boob wouldn't have gone flat and his 1970 Barracuda might not have been wrecked. Hey, I'm all for putting an antidrug message in this book, but I couldn't see the connection.

"There *has* to be an antidrug message in the book," my editor said. "What else are you going to blame everything on?"

"Stupidity?" I asked.

"No, no, no!" she said. "I'm telling you, it's the drugs! I knew a guy who had a friend who smoked some pot and his mother died. What do you think of them apples?"

"*Those* apples," I sighed.

I give up. Okay, I'll say it: *Rastafarians will be the death of us all*. Can we move on now? Because you don't care about all that. You're interested in the fact that Trixie Foxalot was on the prowl.

Her breast was successfully revived, but the greater miracle was that the car was too. Almost everything from the passenger compartment to the front fender was replaced skillfully by a speed shop in Palm Beach. The guy there was impressed with the remains.

"I have a few tricks that will get some more power out of her," he said, "but it won't be cheap."

"Do it," Trixie said, "whatever it costs."

Like Hooter, Trixie realized what she had lost. Of all her men, Hooter had been the most loyal. If she had not been so vain and self-absorbed, she might have seen it then. She certainly knew it now. He had worshipped her, and she had treated him with indifference and distance. A psychologist—a real one, I mean—might suggest that she had pushed him away because then it wouldn't hurt so much when he was gone. All of Trixie's relationships eventually splintered. In Hollywood it seemed normal. Trixie began preparing for the end of each relationship soon after it had begun.

All human beings have some level of decency, so it wouldn't be fair to demonize Trixie Foxalot. Sure, her decency had been buried under a mud slide of Hollywood hedonism. Sure, she was a fraud. She didn't care a whit about world peace. She couldn't have found the Middle East with a map, a microscope, and a tour guide. But

Trixie Foxalot, like us all, needed love. She had distanced herself from it for so long, she had not recognized it until it was gone. That doesn't mean she was a good person or ever would be one, but she was unloved, and that's tragic in any circumstance.

Besides, will you get a load of those knockers.

Within hours, Trixie Foxalot's presence in Sterling, Colorado, had created quite a stir. Ringing phones shared the news. If she had been a minor star before, everyone knew that Trixie was the new "it" girl on *Baywatch*. A real live Hollywood starlet was in town, and she was driving Hooter Pridley's old car.

Everyone at Gladys Neidermeyer's insurance company got the news. Everyone except Gladys. They smiled sadly at her and then giggled wickedly behind her back in the break room. Everyone knew—because Gladys had confided in them—that Hooter had once left her for a picture on a calendar. And now the calendar was back, and Gladys— poor, sweet, innocent Gladys—didn't stand a chance. She was out of her league. They wondered idly if *they* might get close enough for an autograph from Trixie Foxalot.

The girls at Security Life Insurance could have done the decent thing and told Gladys about the approaching collision. Oh, they would tell her, of course, when the joy of knowing something she didn't ran its course. Then they would break the news to her, feigning compassion while watching her squirm. Then they would feel superior and compassionate all at the same time.

Hooter's brother, Zack Pridley, heard the scoop on the radio, and he decided he was damn sure going to see a movie star if there was one this close. He wasn't a big fan, but he had seen her murdered by some Vincent Price wannabe in *Coagulating Screams Unheard* and had found her death impressive and imaginative.

Zack left his ninth beer of the day unfinished on the coffee table and wheeled out with the only limb that wasn't a stump. It took some doing to push the wheelchair along with only one hand. The Veterans Administration kept promising to get him a battery-powered chair, but they never did. But they thanked him every so often for his noble sacrifices in letters that pushed back his next VA hospital appointment by thirty days. It seemed the government wanted Zack Pridley to keep on sacrificing. Although he waited eternally for the battery-powered wheelchair to come, and although he stopped believing in war, Zack Pridley never stopped believing in his government.

The problem with being a one-armed soldier in a wheelchair was that unless he was really on top of his game, and not drunk, it was hard not to spin the thing in circles. But he was a Pridley, and drunk or sober, they are a determined lot.

Zack guessed right. He figured that Trixie Foxalot would find Hooter at Wangdoodle Auto & Truck Parts sooner or later. So he spun inadvertent circles for five blocks to get there.

It was a circus when he arrived. Mechanics from all over town had surrounded Trixie. She smiled and signed autographs as she worked her way inside. The police were called to direct traffic, and a newspaper photographer from the *Sterling Journal-Advocate* was there.

Hooter thought hard about slipping out the back door, but he knew that any woman who had rebuilt his car and driven it halfway across the country would not rest until she saw him face to face. Reluctantly he worked his way forward.

When she saw Hooter, Trixie rushed to him and kissed him passionately. The photographer's camera flashed. In a few seconds, Trixie realized Hooter was not kissing her back. He just stood there, arms at his side, lips tight.

"Hi, baby," she said, "I brought your car back." She dropped the keys into his shirt pocket. "I missed you *so* much. I was a fool, and I want us to be together."

Hooter expected his reaction to be one of ambivalence. But he discovered he really despised her. The intensity of it surprised him. "You're not who you said you were," he said.

"You should talk," she sneered. "I've heard rumors—"

"I have a new life, and this one is real," Hooter snapped. "I'm in love with Gladys, and I'm staying."

Trixie's face hardened. Suddenly she didn't seem pretty at all.

Hooter saw the throng part behind her as a cop cleared the way for Zack Pridley's wheelchair. It was ironic, Hooter thought, that he had fallen in love with Trixie in large part because she *said* she hated war, just like his brother, a man he admired almost as much as his grandfather.

Hooter faced Trixie—plastic, siliconed, liposuctioned, and collagen-injected. Beside her, Zack Pridley sat with three stumps, drunk and unshaven, clutching a pen and pad for an autograph.

Trixie turned to the panting wretch in the chair. "Who's the freak?"

That's how the riot started.

For the first time in his life, Hooter wanted to slap a woman. Maybe even strangle her. He had never struck a woman—not even in grade school—so it's hard to say what he would have done if he had reached her. Greasy-shirted mechanics intervened as Hooter and Trixie shouted unkind things at each other. The mob rolled out into the parking lot as more police arrived. The newspaper photographer snapped wildly.

"Stay here in your hick town with your hick girlfriend," Trixie spat. "You cad!"

That made Hooter even madder. Gladys Neidermeyer was the best person he had ever met. Best of all, she was real.

• • •

Trixie and Hooter were hauled to the police station in separate vehicles. No charges were filed against Trixie, because there is no law against shallow, mean-spirited bimbos—otherwise Los Angeles would be a ghost town. After fulfilling the many requests for autographs at the station, Trixie was ordered to leave town forever or face arrest for slanderously calling the good people of Sterling *hicks*. She contritely promised never to return. An arrest would be a public relations disaster.

"Oh, I'm so sorry, Officer. I don't know what came over me," Trixie said, doing her best Marilyn Monroe breathy voice, which wasn't very good. She sounded like a pro wrestler with asthma.

"Get her out of here," the sergeant said as she was escorted out. "By the way, I loved you in *The Exorcist*."

"And Hooter," the sergeant continued, "what would your grandpa say to all this? It says here in the report that … *Were you really gonna hit her?*"

"I don't know for sure. I don't think so."

"I oughta throw you in jail just for thinkin' about it. Hell and good golly! Didn't your folks raise you better than this?"

"I used to think so," Hooter said, "but I guess not." He had never felt quite so ashamed.

chapter **Forty-Two**

The girls at the office made sure to tell Gladys about Trixie Foxalot an hour before quitting time. They wished they could be there when she caught up with Hooter. They primed her for the conflict by maliciously giving her all sorts of bad advice. Poor Gladys dabbed tears of heartbreak and humiliation.

The girls at the office had advised letting him have it with both barrels, but when Hooter came dragging in at supper time looking so low, Gladys didn't have the heart for it.

"Do you love her?" she asked almost inaudibly, though she knew she could not believe any answer he gave. The girls at the office had told her that.

"No," Hooter said as sincerely as he could. "I love you!"

"But *she* must love *you*!" Gladys sobbed. She had never felt quite so inadequate.

"Not after today," Hooter said.

But nothing he said could console her. He tried. All night he tried, and eventually they were so emotionally spent, they crawled into bed in silence. Gladys could not bring herself to believe that Hooter—or any man—could spurn a woman like Trixie Foxalot for someone like her.

Still, she was comforted by the hours of talking during which he tried to convince her of that impossibility. That had to mean he cared enough about her not to want to crush her completely. It was something. That was the thin thread of hope to which she clung.

But in the morning, she awoke to a nightmare. The front page of the paper showed a picture of Trixie Foxalot's lips locked with Hooter's as her enormous tan breasts flowed out beneath her perfect features. Trixie Foxalot was glamorous, with sparkling diamonds, and she was kissing Hooter with her perfect lips. What woman could compete with that?

Gladys was weeping when Hooter emerged from the bedroom. He saw the tear-stained newspaper and the damning photo.

"Whatever it says, it's not true," he said.

What the article said was that he was Trixie Foxalot's boyfriend. She had told them that. And the story listed all of her accomplishments, all the impressive B movies she had been murdered in and all of the millions of dollars she was making just by jogging on the beach in a swimsuit with David Hasselhoff. They didn't bother citing her measurements. The photo said all that needed to be said. A picture is worth a thousand measurements.

Gladys Neidermeyer couldn't imagine going to work and giving them the satisfaction of seeing her devastation. Hooter didn't much want to see the smirks of the customers at Wangdoodle Auto & Truck Parts either, but he couldn't face a day alone in the house with a weeping Gladys Neidermeyer.

"I am so sorry," he said before he left.

She wiped her eyes and put on a brave smile. "What do you have to be sorry about? She came here. You couldn't help that."

"But, I'm sorry for … for everything."

"I know."

"I love you," he said.

He waited for her response, but it did not come. She could not bring herself to say it. By noon Gladys had almost convinced herself that Hooter loved her enough to make things work out—eventually.

But doubt had a foothold and soon established a beachhead.

Then came the invasion, with doubts parachuting in from the skies. Her positions were overrun.

One who is not in the depths of despair cannot understand the decisions made within it. That despair caused Gladys to do something that no one should ever do. She so desperately sought a confirmation of Hooter's love that she violated a trust. She opened his dresser drawer and pulled out his journal.

There she read the entries that spoke of Hooter's monumental love for Trixie Foxalot. Her beauty. Her intellect. The beautiful soul that sought an end to war. Those magnificent breasts. The full lips. It was crushing. There was no way she could live up to that. Her weeping forced her to stop reading.

But Gladys should have read on. She would have seen the infatuation with Trixie Foxalot fade into disgust. She would have read that Hooter Pridley had completely surrendered his heart to Gladys. But she slammed the book shut without reading that far. Anyway, her tears had begun to soak the pages. In that convoluted state of mind, without knowing all the facts, she devised a solution.

After a day of enduring smirks and wisecracks but mostly whispered inquiries about his sex life with Trixie Foxalot, Hooter staggered into the door, desperate for Gladys's embrace.

"I'm home," he said, tossing his jacket over a chair, even though it bothered Gladys that he didn't hang up his things. "I'm home," he repeated, but by then Hooter had begun to suspect that his voice was all he would hear that night. The house was silent, except for the gurgle of the fish tank.

There was a note on the table.

Dear Hooter, it read, *there's meatloaf warming in the oven. Please feed the fish. And wait for me if you can. I'll be back. I don't know when. I love you.—Gladys. P.S. The garbageman comes on Wednesday. Don't forget to set out the trash.*

● ● ●

Three words in the note kept him hanging on for as long as he did. *I love you.* In the silence of that kitchen, he realized the immense power of those words. Eight letters of the alphabet—arranged in any other way, they meant nothing. But they kept him going in the days to come. More than once he regretted having waited for so long to say those words to Gladys Neidermeyer. He stared at the words on the paper for so long, time seemed to stop.

"I love you, too, Gladys," he said.

But he forgot to feed the fish, and on Wednesday, he forgot to take out the garbage.

chapter Forty-Three

Spring came to Sterling, Colorado, without Gladys Neidermeyer. The grass grew green; the trees burst into an Irish salute. The days went by fast enough for Hooter at the parts store. He had gone from being an object of admiration for his tryst with Trixie Foxalot to being one of pity after Gladys Neidermeyer left him with four goldfish to feed and a better-than-average meatloaf. But by spring, Hooter was no longer admired or pitied. He was just plain old Hooter again. All of that other stuff had been forgotten.

The weekends were long. They would have stretched into eternity if not for Grandpa Pridley, who took Hooter fishing. When the ice melted, they fished the bays in a leaky four-teen-foot Alumacraft with a trolling motor. At times Hooter suspected that Grandpa just brought him along to bail.

Sometimes, Hooter wondered if Gladys really was coming back, or if it was just a cruel vengeance to keep him waiting forever. He would be hard-pressed to blame her if that was what she was doing.

"She'll be back," Grandpa said.

"How can you be sure?" Hooter asked.

"Because she said she would, and she's a Neidermeyer. They're good people."

So Hooter soldiered on, but sometimes he complained about the twists in his life, and he blamed Trixie Foxalot.

Grandpa surmised that Hooter was angry about his discovery that there was no perfect woman, just like every woman figured out that there was no perfect man. Women seemed to catch on to that fact at a much earlier age, because men make it so obvious.

Grandpa Pridley hoped Hooter's anger would fade with time. In the meantime, fishing seemed to be the best medicine. One day Grandpa Pridley showed up with a boat so big, Hooter wasn't sure the lake could hold it.

"My ship came in," Grandpa grinned, because he thought it was pretty funny.

"Strike gold?" Hooter asked.

"Nah. Got a check in the mail. Big one. Out of the blue. From some guy in California named Ben Hor-twit or some such. My share of an advance, he called it."

"Horowitz?"

"That's it. Said he was paying me for my sayings. Guess he put them in a book. Said he split it fifty-fifty. Who'd a believed it? Next thing you know, them bikers are going to send me a check for putting Born to Die on all those T-shirts and tattoos."

Even with the new boat, they caught no fish. But it was fun to watch them pass by on the fish finder.

For the record, Horowitz's book was titled *Things Your Grandpa Would Say*. My favorite was always, "If you've got a toothache, make sure you pull the right one." The book was Horowitz's crowning achievement and was hailed as a new, commonsense approach to psychology. Oprah especially loved it. Hooter's grandfather used the next sizable royalty check to buy a new fish shack, with propane heat and a television.

And let's look in on Horowitz, shall we? Here's how it all played out: Horowitz's wife never returned, but she got more reasonable about the divorce agreement. Van Horn fired Molly McDonald after that incident with the Jackson Pollocks. You probably heard about that. It made all the papers. Letterman couldn't stop talking about it. Molly and Horowitz married, and in time she got less obsessive and he more so—about her. It was quite a lovely romance. They decorated with velvet Elvises.

Van Horn was true to his word—he never exposed Horowitz. And they came to a gentleman's agreement: Van Horn got all the game-show hosts; Horowitz got the rock stars. They split the actors. There was enough insanity to go around.

chapter **Forty-Four**

Hooter's loneliness was like a weight. It grew incrementally heavier with each day. Much of the weight was remorse. It grew worse in the quiet nights alone.

Sometimes, to pass the silent hours, Hooter paged through the stack of magazines that came in the mail with Gladys's name on them. He learned a hundred and one secrets to being a better lover from *Glamour*. He read dandruff tips and the secret to sexier toes. He became an expert on erogenous zones and erotic massage. When Gladys Neidermeyer got home, it was going to be like a science experiment.

But a man can only read so many women's magazines. Hooter visited the Kum and Go newsstand regularly. Mostly he bought *Hot Rod* magazine and *Motor Trend*. But one day another magazine caught his eye. It caused his heart to rise to his throat.

Time magazine had a huge question mark on a screaming red cover. "HOAX EXPOSED?" said the headline. Beneath it read *"Does Helmut Schlossenpfennig really exist?"*

The answer, of course, was no.

It was a huge story. Imagine discovering that Einstein never existed.

It all began to unravel with the untimely death of an obscure Chicago writer who penned magazine articles about pop culture and music. He wrote movie reviews. He raved when Desmond Carson skewered Rico Juarez. He hardly ever left his apartment, let alone Chicago, and his name was Eldrick DeShane. Maybe Eldrick DeShane ran amuck because he never felt loved by his clarinet-playing father, but it's hard to say. Lots of unloved children behave admirably.

When they cleaned out the apartment, authorities did not realize at first the implications of what they had discovered. There were manuscripts everywhere. Under the bed. In the closet. Some had been published. Some were awaiting publication. They were purportedly authored by Helmut Schlossenpfennig.

It was hard to blame the publishers for the outrage that followed. They dealt with eccentric, secretive hermits all the time. That they had never met Professor Helmut Schlossenpfennig face to face did not make the theories any less profound. Not that anyone there understood it, mind you. But the psychiatric community was in awe of the work. So the books kept rolling out, and the secretly puzzled psychologists kept shouting hosannas.

It had all started as a lark.

So much of Eldrick's own work was rejected, he decided to write circuitous nonsense and submit it just for fun. He was astonished when it was accepted, and even more astonished when the royalty checks rolled in.

He served as the agent for the Master of the Mind, of course, and Schlossenpfennig never argued about his cut. The lie got so big, Eldrick became convinced that he would be found out with each new treatise.

The paranoia finally killed him.

He had created something he could not control. He dedicated his life to propping up a man who never existed. Once, he wrote an unauthorized biography on Schlossenpfennig, and it was roundly hooted down. What could a pop culture writer possibly know about such a genius and his methods?

Eldrick DeShane had been proclaimed an icon, but he could not bow to the applause.

Eldrick DeShane never set foot on Sunset Boulevard as his father imagined he might one day. But Eldrick *did* hear his father play. He was a big Zippy Nightshade fan, so when the duets album came out, he snapped up a copy. He heard the lilt of a saxophone on Zippy's duet with Iggy Pop—"Death Sonnet"—but the clarinet is what caught his ear. When Eldrick checked the album credits, he saw his father's name listed as the man behind the saxophone and the clarinet. And Eldrick smiled. A man who made such beautiful music could not be all that bad, he decided.

Artie Shaw heard the album too. He loved Zippy Nightshade.

Luxom DeShane never knew any of that. Maybe inside he felt it. Maybe the angels whisper these things. Maybe Eldrick would have searched out his father, but fate would not allow it. His weak heart gave out while he was listening to his father play.

Eldrick DeShane never knew that he created the man who his father became for a few shining moments at a very good restaurant in Beverly Hills.

chapter **Forty-Five**

There was a bloodletting in the psychiatric community. All those who had so vociferously defended and praised the confusing work of Helmut Schlossenpfennig were exposed as frauds themselves. Among the victims of the witch hunt was poor Van Horn.

Horowitz, who had been so puzzled by the Master of the Mind's work that he never dared speak of it publicly, survived. In the end, he bought the medical plaza back from Van Horn when bankruptcy threatened. You need not shed tears for Van Horn. Horowitz paid market rate, as Molly compassionately advised. And Van Horn's wife stuck by him, even after he had to sell the Porsche.

Hooter was relieved that he had not been implicated in the scandal and that Horowitz went unscathed. But he marveled at how close he had come to destroying the lives around him because of a selfish whim that struck one June and grew to an obsession.

We do not always see the lives we destroy. We do not always see the ones bettered by our actions or by circumstance or happenstance or fate. But someone said—I think it was Einstein—that for every action, there is a reaction. It might have been Mick Jagger.

Hooter Pridley had put something into motion that, despite his newfound good intentions, he could not control. Gladys Neidermeyer was out there, careening about, and he missed her.

chapter *Forty-Six*

June first was a Sunday, and Hooter was glad his grand-father took him fishing to help him forget it was the one-year anniversary of the day he fell in love with Trixie Foxalot. Even his brother, Zack, came along. He fell in once, but for only having one arm, he was a darn good swimmer.

Hooter was pleased when they returned home with no fish, as was their unintentional custom. He hated cleaning the things. He wasn't good at it, because he didn't get much practice. It was good to have his mind on other things, because he had begun to despair of ever seeing Gladys again. The goldfish looked morose, too, and one of them had died. Hooter gave him a funeral in the geraniums.

He eulogized quietly about what a good fish he was, how he never complained and didn't seem to poop as much as the other fish. Maybe he died of constipation. At any rate, Hooter did what Gladys would have: he mourned the fish. This he did to honor her. It was a noble, quietly desperate thing to do. It was the decent thing to do be-cause no one would have known if the fish were simply flushed.

As if on cue, the phone rang after the goldfish funeral. It was the sergeant down at the police station. "Got somebody down here in the holding cell, says she needs to see you."

"Who is it?" Hooter asked. His heart plummeted when he heard the answer.

"Trixie Foxalot," the sergeant said. "I told her we'd arrest her if she came back to town. But she says ... Well, maybe it would be better if you came down here to straighten things out."

"I don't think so."

"Hooter, I'm askin' yuh nice."

"And I'm sayin' *no* nice."

"You want me to haul you in?"

"On what grounds?"

"On the grounds that you're a numskull. Now get in gear."

Hooter drove the Barracuda. Although it was better than before, faster, and the gas gauge worked, he had never felt good about keeping it. He didn't drive it much, just enough to keep the battery charged. It reminded him of Trixie. It would be better if she had taken it with her on her way out of town.

The sergeant raised his eyebrows when Hooter arrived. He led Hooter to the visitor's room. It was empty. A Plexiglas wall separated the incarcerated from the civilians. A line of four black phones hung from the plastic.

The sergeant called for the prisoner by intercom. She came out, escorted by the jailer, and she still looked amazing. You had to notice that. The breasts, the hair, the lips ... Her eyes searched for his, but Hooter could not bring himself to look her in the eye. She sat at the phone and waited for him to pick up the receiver.

Hooter turned to the sergeant. "I can't. Not after everything she's done. I can't even stand to look at her. I'll just put up bail, give her the keys to my car, and that can be the end of it."

"Talk to her," said the sergeant. "Or I'll arrest you, too."

"For what?"

"Failure to answer the phone."

They have some strict laws in Sterling, Colorado.

Hooter reluctantly picked up the phone. He saw her lips move through the Plexiglas, and then he dropped the phone. The voice was not hers. It was the voice of Gladys Neidermeyer.

"It's me," she said after he shakily retrieved the receiver.

Yes, it was Gladys. He could tell by her eyes. Trixie Foxalot's eyes had never been that gentle. My God, what had she done!

She could see that he was horrified. "I did it for you," she said, her voice escalating in cadence as she tried to explain. "I spent everything I had on the surgeries. I thought this was what you wanted," she said. "I would do *anything* for you. Doesn't this prove it?"

Hooter could only moan.

And so the world turns in a year. A man shouts at the gods, and he prays and wishes, and sometimes they maliciously comply. *That's* what I didn't want to tell you. *That's* what I was holding back. Because I like happy endings, and sometimes the truth is more complicated than that. I told you the truth, but I don't feel good about it.

Poor Gladys. Sometimes we work so hard to measure up, we don't stop to consider that maybe we already have.

Gently now, we exit. Maybe it all works out. Maybe it works out in spectacular fashion. I don't know. I never had the will to go back to Sterling, Colorado, to find out. Maybe someday I will.

I can tell you this: one day Hooter got an envelope with oil stock certificates from the Mormon oil well at Noodler's Bluff. But he didn't bother to check their value for a few years, and by then they were worth millions. For a long time Hooter Pridley was rich without knowing it. That's the way it is with some folks.

He ended up with two great cars: the Barracuda and that sleek 1955 Fairlane.

And he had a woman who loved him enough to become someone else.

In the end, Hooter Pridley got everything he had ever asked for.

Acknowledgments

Somewhere in this book, among other philosophies, the narrator opines that a victory doesn't mean much without others to share it with. Without my family—my wife, Julie, and kids, Dylan and India—to celebrate this leg of the journey, it would echo hollow.

Any journey must have direction, so thanks, Mom and Dad, for the example you set. As I was the oldest of six, I remember them being especially eager to point toward the door upon my graduation.

My friend Jane Haas, a longtime English teacher who always did first-run edits on my projects, including this one, is not around to see this one in print, but I am sure somehow, somewhere she is smiling.

I am especially grateful to my agent and friend Connie West, who has worked so hard so my voice may be heard. Sincere thanks to publisher Sam Scinta and Fulcrum Publishing founder Bob Baron for their encouragement. Gratitude is also due to editor Katie Wensuc for her refinements to the manuscript. And I greatly appreciate Erin Palmiter's care and efforts to promote *June*.

Not every worthy voice gets heard. I am grateful to everyone who opened their hearts to mine.

About the Author

Tony Bender grew up in Frederick, South Dakota, a town of four hundred on the border of the Dakotas. That setting provided Bender with a "Tom Sawyer existence" that often surfaces in his writing.

After a radio career "as a professional smart aleck," which included stops at legendary Denver radio stations KHOW and KIMN, Bender began writing professionally. He honed his skills as a popular weekly syndicated columnist in the Dakotas. He was awarded first-place awards for humor writing by the National Newspaper Association in both 2001 and 2002.

Bender was presented the first-ever North Dakota Newspaper Association First Amendment Award (NDNA) in 2000 for his defense of a free press. In 2007, he was elected president of NDNA.

Bender has published three collections of his columns: *Loons in the Kitchen*, *The Great and Mighty Da-Da*, and *Prairie Beat*.

Bender and his wife, The Redhead, have two children, Dylan and India. They make their home on the prairie near Ashley, North Dakota.

Bender can be reached at toploon@yahoo.com or via his website, www.tonybender.net.